Lost in Cooper Park

Also by Libby Sommer and published by Ginninderra Press
My Year with Sammy
The Crystal Ballroom
The Usual Story
Stories From Bondi

Libby Sommer

Lost in Cooper Park

In memory of Roscoe. May you rest in peace in dog heaven.

Lost in Cooper Park
ISBN 978 1 76109 042 4
Copyright © text Libby Sommer 2020
Cover image: Zoya Kriminskaya

First published 2020 by
GINNINDERRA PRESS
PO Box 3461 Port Adelaide 5015
www.ginninderrapress.com.au

Lost In Cooper Park

The tennis courts at Cooper Park in Sydney's east were flooded in the night. One and a half hours of non-stop rain and hail caused a landslide down through the gully. Gypsy, a golden Labrador, came along and splashed in fast-flowing Cooper Creek. Later, the sight of the ruined courts covered in mud and stones, leaves and tree branches like a murky swamp was to shatter Simon's morning.

*

Kingston turned up again on the morning after the storm. He stood on the doorstep looking unbalanced. His cigarette was burned down to the filter. His unshaven face was flecked with grey and white. Crystal wouldn't let him in. He'd misplaced his key a long time ago.

Crystal didn't tell Simon about Kingston being back from Bali and Simon didn't tell Crystal about the tennis courts.

*

The moon was high in the darkening dusk as Rosemary puffed past the tennis courts and up through the steep incline of Cooper Park gully swinging a curved stick with tennis ball.

'Gypsy,' cried Rosemary. 'Gypsy, Gypsy, Gypsy! Come here.'

Rosemary had agreed to adopt Gypsy at her husband's insistence. He'd become worried about how much weight they'd gained since they'd had to put Buddy down. He had strapped the twins into the Nissan and driven to the northern beaches, where an old university friend had kept an animal rescue shelter, and got the dog for nothing. His old university friend was pleased to see another happy animal on his way to a loving family.

Rosemary promised she'd make sure Gypsy didn't jump up on the newly cleaned couches. The puppy looked just like a baby Buddy. Rosemary would have liked to have said it was Buddy reincarnated but didn't. This was precisely the kind of talk that made her husband go red with rage.

He was the one who had named the missing golden Labrador Gypsy. His own name is Philip.

The day would soon be night.

*

Simon lay in bed beside Crystal waiting for the early morning sound of birds. Opening up one of the curtains, he could see down below a car with a person scrunched up across the back seat.

'Don't let anyone in,' demanded Crystal in a dream.

*

Kingston was counting his blessings out loud, although his eyes remained closed. Above his head, he imagined the shapes of the geometric pattern that obsessed him.

He wished he could throttle this dawn awake. He rolled over and stepped out of the car, then began jogging in the direction of Cooper Park.

Four streets away, Gypsy helped himself to the remains of a milkshake beside the sleeping body of a young tattooed female. She lay on a mattress set up on the pavement outside the medical centre.

The street was deserted except for two women. One woman complained to the other, 'She's been sleeping there for the last week and no one does anything about it.'

Crystal gave Simon a pair of secateurs for his birthday so he could do his share of keeping the garden in order. Simon hung them on a hook in the shed out the back. When he came back in, Crystal kissed him.

He kissed her back and ran his hand over her rear end. 'I'll give your bottom a massage later,' he said.

Crystal had been complaining about a pain, probably a pulled muscle, on the side of her spine and into her hip. They always had sex on birthdays. Simon sighed deeply, shoulders slumped. Crystal knew better than to say anything. Simon tended to get emotional on his birthday because, no matter how many people sent a text or emailed, he always felt unloved.

*

Eight-year-old Priscilla scowled at Simon as she unwrapped the surprise toy he'd bought her at the newsagent. 'It didn't cost that much money,' she whinged. 'I've got that one already. Have you got a pen? I'll tick off the ones I've got.'

He handed her a four-colour pen.

She set the Shopkins promotional poster out on the floor and turned her back on him. 'No. None of my friends can swap with me. We're not allowed to bring toys to school. No. I can't swap with them in after-school Chinese lesson, or at the swim class. We can't take toys to school.'

'Maybe Mummy could bring the Shopkins doll in the car when she picks you up.'

'When will my mummy be home?'

The storm clouds thickened the sky.

*

Priscilla sobbed during her shower and her fish fingers and chips. Simon thought it must be because a thunderstorm was brewing, but it turned out that while she'd been playing near the tennis courts in Cooper Park that afternoon, a teenager with tattooed arms had stepped out from one of the man-made caves and said, where are you off to, sister? Simon said Priscilla was too young to be going out the front gate alone.

'She's a very sensible girl. No need to be a helicopter parent,' said Crystal.

Crystal had a dark shadow of chocolate sullying the top of her lipstick-red mouth. Her mobile started its chanting.

'Why don't you answer your phone these days?' asked Simon.

'It's nobody,' said Crystal.

*

Simon was having his missed-the-flight dream again.

His new lightweight suitcase, long enough to hold his tennis racket, had been so overloaded he couldn't zip it up.

'Breath in for three and out for three,' insisted a man in a turban.

Simon felt a tightening sensation move down to his stomach and woke up. A full moon edged its beam through a gap in the curtains revealing a pile of deflated soccer balls on the floor. Each had been returned 'address unknown'. He'd ripped up the packaging and refused to give up hope.

That's all he could do. Hang on to hope for a reconciliation with his son.

That morning, in the newspaper, his horoscope had said the full moon would have a message for him.

He sat up and pressed the remote button to turn the fan off. That's what the moon was trying to tell him, that he could stop the noisy cold draft blowing across the back of his neck.

*

Looking for Gypsy.

Priscilla balanced on the thick ropes strung above the slippery dip in the children's playground in Cooper Park while Simon stood combing his hair with his fingers. His thick mane made him feel virile and attractive, and handsome enough to catch the attention of a woman who walked towards him and asked if he'd seen her golden Labrador.

'We've met at tennis,' said Simon.

'Maybe,' said Rosemary, flicking her braided plait across her shoulder.

*

Kingston was using the free WiFi in the shopping centre to make contact with Crystal. 'We need to tell Priscilla the whole story about her big sister running away with the tennis coach,' he rehearsed to himself. He needed to get through to explain his retreat to Bali.

The phone kept going straight to voicemail. A child needed to know why her father couldn't hack life in the city after the disappearance of his first born.

A man in a white shirt sat down opposite him. The man gestured to the newspaper on the table.

Kingston nodded. Sure, take it.

*

Looking for Gypsy.

It was after five when Simon brought Priscilla home.

Crystal was concerned. 'You know how long it takes to give her dinner, bath and into bed,' she scowled, unclasping the Velcro on Priscilla's sandals. A few tiny pebbles landed on the tiles. 'Where've you been?'

'Looking for a missing golden Labrador,' Simon told her.

*

The cat sat in the laundry basket on top of the clean clothes. Simon was upstairs running a bath for Priscilla. Crystal sat at her desk in the lounge room, catching up on the latest social media news.

Rain water poured out the guttering at an angle, spluttering in through the loft window while Kingston quietly slid the skylight open and climbed inside.

Usually, Crystal climbed up a ladder and gave the gutters a clean out so the rain wouldn't splash in. Perhaps more of the copper edging had broken off. The dormer windows were surrounded by masking tape. She had taped them before they painted the loft, although Simon had said, 'Don't bother. I'll scrape the paint off after.'

Kingston was like most guys his age. He'd hardly picked up a hammer.

'You were built for decoration only,' Crystal had laughed at him when the two of them had talked about renovating. A bit of encouragement wouldn't have gone astray instead of, 'You missed a bit,' or 'I wouldn't have painted it this colour.'

Kingston ran his hand along the wall and clicked the light on.

She'd got rid of his exercise bike and his Balinese *objet d'art*. She'd put in a couch, a kitchenette and a tiny bathroom. She must be making a packet in that job. That useless mongrel Simon wouldn't be bringing in anything. For sure, he'd moved himself in and was sleeping on his, Kingston's, side of the bed.

He looked around for something to throw at the wall or, better still, at Crystal's Venetian glass collection.

Although he had nearly fallen off the ladder that he'd dragged out from the storeroom under the house, he was feeling more grounded, more secure. He put it down to the guy in the white shirt who'd handed him the shiny flyers that could change his life. Also, he'd shaved off his flecked-with-grey beard and looked ten years younger.

*

Still looking for Gypsy.

When she discovered the gap in the skylight and the rainwater on the floor, Crystal thought the best thing to do was tell Simon that Kingston had given up his home in Bali and returned to Sydney. 'Not wanting to repeat myself,' she said, spraying a cockroach on the wall and another on the benchtop, 'but what makes me the angriest is his total lack of responsibility regarding Priscilla. Running off like that to sit with his guru, and me about to give birth. It's not as if I wasn't suffering as much as him – you know, after Zoe's disappearance. Thank god for Priscilla. What is this? I can't read the tiny writing.'

Simon took the dog-eared flyer Crystal had found under the kettle and read, 'In Search of the Miraculous. Meetings with remarkable men…'

'Oh, for goodness sake,' said Crystal. 'Really, I've had more than enough of all that stuff.'

So had Simon. Instead, he thought of Rosemary. 'We should get a guard dog, you know. But not one of those little yappy things.'

'And who would take the dog for a walk? Twice a day. But I will get some proper locks for the windows. Okay?'

Simon said locks wouldn't make much difference if someone really wanted to break in, but Crystal was plugged into her audiobook already.

*

Still looking for Gypsy.

Rosemary had more children than she had energy for. Twin toddlers and a teenage girl. She didn't need any more people in her life who required constant attention or help with planning their life's path.

In spite again of his denials, she knew Simon had only wanted to meet to show her the café where he liked to sit and write his poetry so he could ask her to give him feedback on his poems.

She'd been in a strange state when she'd made the mistake of accepting his invitation to join him at the art gallery, she thought glumly as she walked across the grass of the botanic gardens to meet him. When was she going to learn to say 'no'? She could see him standing on the steps in wait for her.

Simon swung his daypack on to his shoulder and focused on her approaching figure. He liked what he saw. 'Homely' would be the best word to describe her. He'd always said it was women who'd had children that attracted him the most. Good listeners. Understanding personalities. Respect for Rosemary's feminist sensibilities stopped him from staring at her boobs.

By the time they'd walked around the gallery and were sitting in the bar enjoying a drink, Rosemary let herself recreate that day in Cooper Park when he'd helped her in the search for Gypsy. There was a limit to what she was prepared to do in return. It's not as if they'd found the golden Labrador, but Simon had struck her as a dalliance she might fancy.

Simon grinned at her tentatively and sipped his schooner. Rosemary reminded herself that she had no intention of emailing or texting him to the numbers he'd written down for her. Who had the time? She had to find Gypsy before the children went into deep grieving. She'd been long enough at the art gallery. She had dinner for the family to think about.

*

Priscilla rummaged in her mother's pyjama drawer for the hidden stash of lollies she'd taken out of the tin in the drawer in the kitchen. She popped a whole chocolate frog into her mouth. Judiciously, she slipped a packet of Lifesavers into her pocket for later and closed the zip.

She strolled outside in search of a friend to play with.

Ten minutes later, her mother saw her from the TV room trying to unlatch the front gate that separated the lawn from the driveway.

Seeing her so purposeful made Crystal want to run out and kiss her. She felt an unfamiliar glow of pride, a sense of ease in their mother/daughter relationship that she did her best to acknowledge with gratitude. Sometimes, regularly in fact, Crystal would have liked to talk about her feelings of inadequacy as a parent with Simon, but Simon seemed to think he had priority over discussions about feeling inadequate in life, and didn't want to share the available airtime. Crystal frowned. Even with those feelings of not being up to the job of mother, she considered herself a very stable person, unlike Simon, who was all over the place. Highs and lows. Totally unpredictable. Just how unpredictable she didn't know yet. Their life together had barely unfolded. Everyone she knew was a bit of a worry anyway. It was just a matter of where on the spectrum a person was situated.

Priscilla was no longer in the front garden.

Crystal hoped Simon would get home in time to do the shopping. There was nothing in the house for dinner.

*

Simon had walked through the botanic gardens to calm and ground himself in the colour green after Rosemary's harsh criticism of his latest poem. Then, on the train going home, he'd given some deep thought to his friendship with Rosemary. As an editor of her company's newsletter, among other things, she seemed a suitable person to help him get a poem published in the *Canberra Times*. The next deadline was less than a week away. On second thoughts, he decided not to mention anything about Rosemary being a possible writing mentor to Crystal, who had already set the bar very low by being so evasive about Kingston's whereabouts.

*

Simon and Crystal needed to discuss their financial situation.

Simon thought Crystal's plan to convert the room under the house into a self-contained studio with kitchen and bathroom to be an excellent idea. Crystal had realised that even having a second job was not enough to keep up with the mortgage repayments. Mr and Mrs Clifton next door would have to be persuaded not to object to a building application.

The thing was, Simon wasn't exactly a huge contributor to the household expenses. He rented a chair in a hairdressing salon and worked part-time as a hairdresser.

Crystal reminded him it wasn't all that long ago that she'd spoken to the bank manager and increased her overdraft. She would love to have some extra money to spend on selfcare for herself and to have a pedicure from time to time, just like her girlfriends did.

What's more, she'd been able to save money on their telephone and WiFi bill by signing up for a landline ADSL bundle that was the same price as she'd been paying for just the landline.

Crystal wasn't overly confident that, as their lives unfolded together, their finances would automatically improve. Simon shook his head. He was a great believer in the saying that two could live more cheaply than one.

*

Kingston caught the bus to Balmain for the meeting in the dingy room at the top of the stairs. Things were working out. He'd been accepted into this Gurdjieff group and saw no need to start his own in the east, but he wished he could bed down from time to time in Crystal's shed on the other side of the backyard pool.

Kingston crossed the room and found a spare cushion to sit on. These new-found friends with a common interest were just what he needed. The meditation would do him good. He needed to learn to focus again. He found comfort in the silence.

*

Coca Cola had just disclosed the fourteen health experts who'd taken cash.

After reading this, Simon frowned at Crystal over the top of the *Sydney Morning Herald*.

He needed his daily sugar hit.

He wanted to drink plenty of beer too, preferably full strength.

He wanted hamburgers and hot dogs and ice cream for dessert every night.

He wanted lots of things. He was one of those people who always wanted more. Never satisfied.

Simon struggled to see the big picture; considered saving money to buy a car, a thought that promptly tipped him into a panic attack.

'Oh, for goodness sake,' said Crystal reaching for the tin of Rescue Remedy jubes. 'What's the matter now?'

'It's hard to verbalise.' And it was. Life should be fair and balanced like the rhyme and rhythm of a couplet poem, that's all.

'Here's the thing,' said Crystal, tapping the page with a honeyed ladle. 'Just have a look at this. It says here that one of the professors told Coke the association with type 2 diabetes was real and causal.'

'That's old news,' said Simon.

'They said Coke needs to reduce serve sizes.'

'As if,' said Simon.

'Well-being partners is what they call them. Coke funded the Global Energy Balance Network who said that health policy combating obesity should focus on exercise rather than controlling dietary intake.'

'Outrageous. We all know that body size is eighty per cent to do with what you eat.'

'You can stop those early morning jogs.'

'Ha, ha. The thing is, you still have to move.'

'We all know sitting is the new smoking.'

*

'Being upfront is the best policy,' said Simon. 'I enjoy the company of in-telligent, interesting women, more so than that of men. Bit weird, hey?' '

At first, it had felt like love. Him and Crystal. Becoming good friends, that maturing of a relationship, might happen later.

'Yes, I know all that. You told me already.'

*

In Priscilla's room, a large multilevel doll's house, made of wood and filled with tiny wooden furniture, took up half of one wall. Crystal was always telling her to tidy out its rooms that had accumulated bits and pieces of jewellery, hair ribbons, pens and pencils, but she rarely got around to it. Priscilla had set up a bed for the cat on its ground floor. Wondering where the cat bedded down at night, Crystal went into the room where Priscilla was colouring in on the floor. Crystal saw her best silk scarf lining the cat's bed. She told Priscilla that if she ever went through her drawers again while she was out at work, she would be severely punished.

Priscilla nodded. 'What belongs to me doesn't belong to you,' she said in a sing-song voice.

'Would you believe it?' Crystal said to Simon later. 'Where do you think she gets these ideas from?'

She got it from the Homeless Girl, who had let her have a taste of her Coke when Priscilla had admired its fizz.

*

Sometimes the Homeless Girl let Priscilla play with her giant teddy bear. Priscilla wanted to borrow the bear even though she had a whole shelf of them at home.

The Homeless Girl lived in a man-made cave in Cooper Park on the other side of the street, or sometimes she'd bed down under the tarpaulin of one of the boats attached to a trailer that lined the road to the Cooper Park tennis courts car park. It was Priscilla's deepest secret that this girl really was her sister, the one who was never to be mentioned. It would set Mummy off with the most awful sobbing.

But Simon knew none of this and so didn't answer Crystal's question about where Priscilla got her ideas from, and anyway Crystal believed in helping those less fortunate than herself, especially teenagers who couldn't find their way in life.

*

Once upon a time, so it is said, in a wintertime which was exceptionally mild, when the domestic situations in the 1980s were not dissimilar to today, six-year-old Kingston, all by himself after school, answered the telephone.

The man said it must be a wrong number and asked Kingston his name. The man stayed on the line chatting in a friendly manner for a very long time, his voice smooth and silky. The voice made Kingston feel all warm and sleepy and made him long for his dad, still serving time for petty crimes in Long Bay jail.

After that, the man rang most afternoons after school and spoke to Kingston of strange things. On the man's instructions, Kingston pretended to do things to himself on the other side of the phone. The man suggested they meet up one day soon and that Kingston could watch people doing things to each other.

Kingston had not told his older brother about the phone calls. Anyway, Clark was meant to be at home with him keeping an eye on things. One day when Clark had got back earlier than usual, he asked Kingston who was on the phone. He shouted at Kingston and Kingston had shouted back and then their mum had come home and told them to bring the shopping in from the car.

'Why were you yelling at him, Clark? What've you been saying?' she wanted to know, and all in that voice like a knife, long and sharp that terrified Kingston. Someone would be in for it.

His mother had smacked his brother, who'd turned red except for the outline of her fingers in white across his face, and he'd slapped her back, and then she'd slapped him again and again. Then she'd reached out to Kingston and brushed back his mop of hair from his forehead and told him to go outside and play.

'Don't put me in this position,' he'd heard Clark yell from the top of the stairs. 'You shouldn't do this to me. I don't want to be the man of the house.'

Kingston hadn't wanted to be outside playing while his brother was sobbing in his room. But he'd opened the back door and gone out anyway.

*

Simon stood under the shower shaving his face and neck, ruminating about the foolish decisions he'd made in his life. His son, for instance. The teenage Lawrence, still angry, still living with his mother, Doctor Sarah in France. He mourned him every day when he inflated one of those returned soccer balls from upstairs and kicked it around the backyard with Crystal's girl, Priscilla.

*

The constant coming and going of cars delivering children to the tennis courts at Cooper Park for lessons after school had ceased by six p.m.

A camper van – dreamcatchers hanging from the windows and sea shells lined up along the back seat – glided to a stop outside Number 18 Cooper Park Road. Kingston in a white loose caftan over pale blue jeans eased himself from the passenger seat. He stepped lightly in his sandals up the front path, brick in hand, and drew his arm back when he reached the leadlight sitting room windows and aimed at Crystal's Venetian glass collection. The camper van pulled out from the gutter as Kingston ran down the footpath and hurled himself back in beside the driver, a young woman with long dreadlocks. 'Capitalist pigs,' she mumbled. The car turned right at the gym, veered to avoid a girl and a dog about to cross the road and sped away in the direction of the shopping centre.

Kingston brought to mind what used to be his leadlight windows framed by fold-back shutters. He thought with sadness about the new bright white paint, although the stark white made the house look like a Greek villa.

The brick had flung itself out of his hand, shot forward like a bullet to shatter the glass but stopped short of the display cabinet.

The shattering, followed by shouting, had disturbed the quiet street. Kingston made his escape as bits of glass continued to fall from behind the newly painted blue window shutters.

*

Priscilla, who was allowed to use a knife now, smeared lumps of Vegemite across her toast. 'Mass destruction,' she muttered at Simon, who wasn't listening to her, his attention struggling to hear what Crystal had been confessing to the next-door neighbour at the front door.

He looked past Priscilla, down the hallway to the spare bedroom, where a pile of crochet beanies were spread out on the bed. Crystal worked on her crochet charity projects every night in front of the tele. She was proud of her contribution to the local community. She had crocheted blanket squares, beanies and doilies and was very satisfied with her colour combinations.

In the winter, the couch was piled high with colourful balls of wool and ergonomic crochet hooks in various sizes and now the only ball visible was the white connecting colour that would pull all the blanket squares together.

'Crash, crash,' chanted Priscilla, her hands in the air.

'Keep your voice down,' reprimanded Simon.

The all-seeing-neighbour left after giving Crystal a description of the camper van and Crystal came back in.

'So?'

'It was probably Kingston. You know what he's like. I just have to put up with his histrionics.'

'Nothing to do with me,' said Priscilla.

Crystal smiled and stroked the girl's cheek. 'No. Nothing to do with you, sugar plum,' she said.

*

In the south of France, Doctor Sarah clutches at her pillow behind the lace curtain of her antique mahogany bed. She has her own story about the break-up, inspiring dreams so scary she wakes with an aching jaw. She kicks the sheet down to her ankles to cool down and to feel the breeze through the window. It's so hot in the summer. High humidity moistens her face, saturates her T-shirt, dampens her hair, causes her throat to close up, causes large waves to break on the shore as though the whole world was stretching out there on the sand in front of her.

She throws her towel down and he spreads his out next to her. The skin on her back is burning, but he will not apply the sunscreen; he says she needs to toughen up. The undersides of her feet burn as she links her foot around his on the sand, frowning with blistered lips into his face. The knife is in her hand. Really? Where did that come from? She makes as if to speak words of love to her own once-beloved husband. And so, remembering the days when they'd still been in love, she stabs him and wakes to find the sky a clear cloudless blue. Like the morning he'd taken off, telling her he was just going out to the car to look for his phone.

Doctor Sarah has never given up hope in the search for true love. Simon has always held on to a vision of finding 'the one'.

*

The first thing Kingston noticed after hopping out of the escape van and relaxing in a café with a flat white, was the variation of the muted earthy tones of the brick wall in front of him. He looked out through the glass to a myna bird standing on one of the ceiling cross beams, its yellow beak darting here there and everywhere.

He watched for a moment, his lips pressing together in concentration. Then he opened the door and went to ask directions from the barista at the front of the café who, as things turned out, knew exactly how to get to the Beverly Springs Wellness Centre. She gave him the bus number and location of the bus stop and, as Kingston turned to cross the road, called, 'Be careful what you wish for.'

She didn't mean the traffic on the busy road but meant the new-age-speak of the place he was headed.

*

Still looking for Gypsy.

Crystal and Simon meandered across to the café in Cooper Park in search of lunch. They were celebrating having a day to themselves, thanks to Crystal's dad, and the fact Crystal's Venetian glass collection had remained intact, although the windows had needed to be replaced.

Almost every table in the café beside the tennis courts was occupied.

Simon caught a glimpse of Rosemary as she missed a wide serve by a left-hander to the backhand court.

'What will you have?' asked the waitress.

Rosemary looked up from the court and noticed Simon. Who was he with? A real person. Not a Helen Hodgman character. An angular dark-haired beauty, narrow face, narrow eyes. A person who took life too seriously, you could see it in the set of her jaw. She was frowning now as she turned a glossy page of a glossy magazine.

Rosemary stared as the thoughtful brunette, head inclined towards the audacious slicked-back one, stared at the hollow-cheeked deliberate kiss planted on the unshaven waiting cheek. Mm. Did Simon have a significant other? she wondered, picking a ball up with a flick of the side of her foot. A woman who called a spade a spade, she thought.

Should she go over and say hello to Simon, be introduced to the woman? But she missed her chance. By the time the last point of the set was played, they'd gone.

*

Priscilla peered through the branches of the shrubs and in through the grey glass of the abandoned car's window, there in the Cooper Park parking area. Was she in there?

Through the leaves she saw the line of white powder on the car's dashboard. She saw the bright orange plastic straw that, days ago, she'd taken from the kitchen drawer. She saw the treasured Homeless Girl pinch one of her nostrils closed, then stick the straw up the other nostril before leaning over the dashboard. Why's she doing that? A straw up her nose? She watched the white stuff disappear as the girl snorted loudly.

Priscilla sucked in her breath.

*

Crystal had heard that Kingston was back in Newcastle living in a friend's spare room. She was pleased he'd been taken in. She hoped he'd settle down. She felt settled with Simon as they embraced on the Rose Bay ferry wharf where boats were unhooked from car trailers and lowered into the water. Vibrant sun between thick white clouds beamed patches of brightness on them, his arms squashing her breasts to his chest, his erection pressed against her thigh. Settled.

*

Philip looked up from his computer when Rosemary walked in.

She kissed him on the back of the neck. 'How's it all going?'

'Grace says she's loving her holiday in Melbourne,' he said.

'She loves wet and cold?'

'You know what she's like.' Philip logged out, rolled back in his chair and took a sip from the Scotch on the rocks in the cut-crystal glass on the leather-tooled desktop.

'I wish you wouldn't start up so early in the day.'

'I know.'

'I think I'll see if I can make a date with her to Skype. She never answers my emails.'

'She needs to rebel,' Philip's eyebrows moved towards each other to meet in the middle, 'to push us away. It's a normal part of growing up.'

'But how come she's not like that with you?'

'She is sometimes. It's the mother–daughter thing with you. She's not the daughter you'd hoped for, and you're not the kind of mother she wanted.'

'Is that so, sweetheart?'

'It's not as if we can ground her now she's all the way down in Melbourne.'

'Kids!'

*

Crystal checked on her own darling daughter asleep in a bed full of teddy bears and then went to see if any more emails had come in from work.

Simon was asleep on the couch, in front of the television. Crystal came in and turned on the light above her desk. They were a contented couple. Crystal typed in her password.

Soon the only sounds were the click of the keyboard, which were intermittent as she searched for the relevant numbers to key in.

She was pleased with her expertise in Excel. There was never a shortage of contracts on offer.

She looked across at Simon. When Simon was involved in things – usually when he was cooking or playing with Priscilla – he seemed happy with the world. Crystal adored him, warts and all. They hadn't known each other that long, but things seemed to be working out.

*

Still looking for Gypsy.

Gypsy, out of sight, digs up the faeces from the cat's litter and eats them.

*

Kingston had been ten when his brother told him they weren't true brothers. He was devastated. He didn't know their mother had been married before. Why hadn't anyone told him? Clark took the bawling Kingston to their mother to have the facts validated. His mother said she'd intended waiting until he was older before telling him these things. She'd half scared him to death talking about how girls could get pregnant by sitting on a toilet seat after a boy had been there. She reckoned she didn't really know how babies were made when she fell pregnant at fifteen. She'd married a second time when she was thirty-five.

Why had his mother had another child so late in life?

'I had no idea, son. I had no idea your father would want more children.'

And the next day his father had been taken away to prison.

'It's a man's world,' was what his mother had said to explain Kingston's existence.

*

Coming back from her early morning swim in the Mediterranean, Peter Garrett singing his heart out in her ears, Doctor Sarah (*la Doctoresse de Anti-ageing*) discovers a familiar-shaped package leaning against her front door. It has the proportions and shape of a football and is stamped with pictures of Australian plant species. The meditative state induced by the swim disappears. *La Doctoresse* flings the iPod out of her ears. Peter Garrett and Midnight Oil shatter on the stylish French entrance tiles.

Inside the apartment, Lawrence is sanding down the wall of his bedroom while watching television and, as one program ends and another begins, is exposed to a documentary on assisted dying so powerful and distressing he puts his sanding mitten down and turns the screen towards him. The strangled sobbing of her golden boy sends a stab of terror into his mother's solar plexus like the shot of a gun and propels her fast as a bullet into his room.

Sanding down the wall again, Lawrence keeps his back to the television images, aware of the long-lasting effect of distressing visuals on his psyche, but unaware of his mother's overwhelming urge to protect her offspring from the harsh realities of life.

Peter Garrett's words of power and passion reverberate from the iPod on the floor.

La Doctoresse turns off the television and flops on her son's bed as Lawrence explains it was a particularly sad bit and not an over-reaction to the state of the walls.

The hideous guilt of the separation from her son's father beats to the same relentless rhythm as the iPod. Will she be feeling guilty forever? Will she never be rid of the connection with Simon? Maybe he'll have a heart attack and die an early death and she'll finally be free of him.

*

Vicki. Oh yes. Vicki. What's this about all of a sudden? wonders Simon. A change of season, a testosterone surge, what exactly?

It was a plane. Flying to Cairns for an island honeymoon. Years and years ago. Dry and dehydrating in the cabin, as it was then and still is these days, and him calling for an air hostess.

That morning he'd packed up his wedding tux (he'd get the hotel to send it back to the hire place), and, with time to fill before their flight, he'd suggested they go visit her parents. And then she'd sobbed he hadn't even wanted to spend the first morning of their married life with her. And she said he hadn't even made love to her on their wedding night, and he'd paid no attention to her at the wedding reception, hardly danced with her at all.

Things had calmed down again but then twenty-one-year-old boy-husband Simon, easing back with a cold beer in his hand, said to the air hostess, 'Can you get a glass of water for the girl next to me.' He'd found himself unable to say the words 'my wife'.

He'd tilted his economy seat all the way back and closed his eyes. His 'cute little package' is how he'd described her in his wedding speech. It surprised him that her father had given the okay. Simon's eighteen-year-old child-bride. Surely things would work out when they got used to each other. 'You get out of life what you put in,' his father had said. It wasn't something Simon wanted to hear.

On the honeymoon, they'd argued. He'd wanted to be up and out early doing stuff, she'd wanted to stay in bed and make love.

But then she'd gone for a dive off Agincourt Reef, a hundred kilometres north of Cairns. He'd decided to snorkel elsewhere that day. He'd waited and waited in their motel room for her to return. Eventually, when he turned the television on, he heard about a tragedy on the news: 'Woman dead after scuba diving incident off Great Barrier Reef'. She'd been on her second dive for the day when she was found on the ocean floor with her regulator out of her mouth. A nurse on board the tour vessel tried to revive her with a defibrillator, a spokesman for Queensland Ambulance said. An emergency helicopter dropped a doctor on board but after an extended effort with no response she was declared dead on the scene.

The small black wire cage that held the salt and pepper grinders, the Tabasco and the sugar that Crystal had made in the industrial design class fell to bits on the floor, sugar spilling out everywhere as he reached for his coffee.

He gave a deep-throated croak of self-loathing, pulled out a hand-

kerchief, blew his nose with a loud honk. He felt his gut grip with regret, naive decisions of the past burning their way from his stomach to
his throat.

*

Still looking for Gypsy.

The Love-Your-Shape (for women with curves) Intimate Apparel
trainees, arrived for their meeting by train, bus, SUV and by duco-bat-
tered BMWs.

'16DD, 14C, 12B,' whispered Simon as he ticked the women off
in his head, watching from behind the curtain in the spare room.

A rusty blue Nissan Pulsar pulled up out the front. Simon stepped
back from the window. He recognised the male stylist. He was the one
from Katoomba, who reckoned he'd known him at school. For God's
sake. Can't a bloke be anonymous in his cave?

Simon had spent a long time re-creating himself and didn't want to
be reminded of the bad old days. Simon would surely remember being
in the same rugby team as a lanky ginger-headed maths whizz named
Julian. There weren't too many of them in Katoomba.

Simon watched while what's-his-name rummaged about in the boot
of his car, pulling out a storage box and a clothes rack which he wheeled
up the driveway, crushing the gravel under his shiny red leather shoes,
purchased online.

Crystal had provided that detail.

Crystal had been madly in love with this Julian person for a long
time when she was younger. But her parents had split them up, saying
she was too young to have a serious boyfriend.

The front door creaked closed behind Julian and the clothes rack.

Simon's wrist was aching from holding back the heavy curtain. RSI
from all those hours cutting and styling hair. He used his left hand to
pull back his right towards his inner elbow to give it a stretch and decided
to go out and look for his new friend Rosemary, who'd lost her dog.

*

Still looking for Gypsy.

Rosemary saw him coming: saw his RM Williams boots stomp down the sizzling pavement, the deliberate tight fit of his shirt gripping his chest to reveal the outline of his biceps, his quick smirk as he saw her sitting against the cushions in the window seat of the café opposite the bicycle shop on Bronte Road.

In he came. He peeled off his black cotton shirt and revealed a tight white singlet and patched-at-the-knee jeans, no doubt rescued from Vinnies. He pulled out a chair and thumped down opposite her. 'So?' he wanted to know.

He's got a beautiful mouth, she thought. She allowed herself a brief glimpse of him flat on his back on the fake wood floor beneath them, his singlet and jeans ripped off, the feel of his hands gripping her butt as she rose and fell above him.

'Yes, please,' said Simon to the friendly waitress as she offered them a decanter of water. And to Rosemary, 'So what are you going to do then?'

'About what?"

'That dog of yours that you've lost.'

'Philip is furious.'

'It's not your fault Gypsy ran away.'

'Philip thinks differently.'

'We can go back to Cooper Park and start looking for him again.'

Rosemary felt a bit better. A problem shared is a problem halved, as the saying goes. The twins were obviously too young to be of any help. Grace was too self-absorbed. Philip never left his desk. The police weren't particularly interested. As usual, if she didn't go the extra mile to look after Gypsy, nobody would.

Simon kept steady eye contact with her even as he bit into a slice of banana bread. 'You haven't got a problem with me joining in the search, have you?'

'Of course not,' said Rosemary, feeling relieved already. 'It's very kind of you to offer.'

Just what was going through his mind? The rise of the corner of his mouth again. Was he plotting something? It reminded her of Philip when he'd direct his gaze away from her, more interested in what was going on around them. He wasn't one for conversation; well, not with her anyway. Yes, that's what it was. That awful feeling of invisibility.

Simon leaned across the table towards her. Rosemary sucked in a breath then giggled. She moved her body across the table to meet him halfway, slipped his hand inside her blouse so he could feel the fullness of her breast. Simon did not take his hand away. He looked back at her.

The waitress was looking at her too. She told them to get the hell out of there if that's what they were up to. So they left the café.

*

Doctor Sarah and her husband Simon leave Prince of Wales Hospital where their son, the young Lawrence, had been rushed earlier that morning to have his tonsils removed and his nose cauterised. He lies peacefully now, blood-free and without distress, clutching his teddy bear, his eyes closed, while his mum and dad tiptoe out of the room and into the waiting elevator. They kiss with relief all the way down to the parking station.

They find their way to the rock pool at the beach, where they cleanse away their worries and continue comforting each other while weight-less.

They dry off along the cliff path that leads through the cemetery with its panoramic ocean views. They stop to read the headstones. She wants to go home, but not yet, for Simon places her hand at the front of his jeans and unzips his fly. He wants her, he says. Here, now, on top of the cliffs above the beach. He pulls her down beside him across the grass-covered grave. He moves her swimmers out of the way between her legs, slips himself in from the side.

And afterwards when she's snapped her swimmers back into place and straightened up, he's still lying there with his fly open, the sun sparkling on his penis in pearly drops like a cover of dew in the warm morning air, as waves foam onto the shore below. She takes his penis and folds it away. His zip makes stuck sounds as it catches on his damp speedo but then the zipper slides quite easily, leaving nothing behind. He brushes the dirt and twigs from her back and hair, laughing, so joyously that she has to fasten his black leather belt herself and hug him to deaden the noise lest the walkers along the cliff path by the sea in their joggers and sun visors look up and are forced to draw attention to a sign which reads, RESPECT FOR THE DEAD: DO NOT WALK ACROSS THE GRAVES.

*

It was at the same hotel in Cairns where they'd overnighted on the way to the Great Barrier Reef.

The housemaid banged on the door, alerted by reception that it was way past check out time and there'd been no sign of the couple in Room 207. She found him feverish and hallucinating on the bed, the underside of his right foot showing a worrying flesh wound.

'I'll never get to make things up to her,' Simon sobbed to the paramedic who came to disinfect and bandage his wound. 'I won't get another chance.'

'Well, we never know what the future holds, do we, love? It's in the hands of the gods.' This woman has attended to many unsuspecting tourists spiked by tiny marine jellyfish stingers or cut by the sharp edges of the coral reef. 'You never know what's around the corner. Just remember how precious life is.'

'I'll never love again,' says Simon desperately.

'Time is a great healer,' says the paramedic.

When his bride's body is brought back to Sydney and the dive company deposits a large sum into the widower's bank account and after Simon begins to emerge from the shadows of grief, he retrains as a hairdresser, joins Youth Hostels, throws on a backpack and heads off to explore the world.

*

It was a glorious morning. The sun, rising above the ridgeline of the gully, slowly warmed the sky to magnificence. Autumn seemed on the cusp of crisping into winter, the sky above Cooper Park gully streaked with cinnamon.

Crystal stood on top of the extension ladder, all-seeing and pensive, both hands gripping the top rung. She'd checked the skylight. All seemed to be in order.

One of the sashes on the old kitchen windows had broken and the window had jammed open at the top. She'd hammered a nail in to seal it closed. There'd be no more moths flying in at night, and no more un-invited visitors.

The hard physical work of wielding the hammer to drive the nails in, of climbing up and down the ladder, had released the tension from the effort needed to absorb last night's training session and she hoped she'd have the energy to get herself to work.

Crystal often felt exhausted, especially after eating frozen meals bought from the supermarket laden with additives. Junk food, as Simon liked to say. It was a battle to juggle her job and to train as a stylist for the Women With Curves range, and deal with the back-stabbers who made life extra difficult.

That snake-in-the-grass Dina, for instance, appearing from nowhere, laying down the law, bossing everyone around, taking Priscilla's colour-ing-in book on the grounds it stifled creativity and shouting when Priscilla kicked her and Crystal made her give it back.

Who did Dina think she was? Some kind of hippy from Nimbin (threesomes, blended families) who'd returned to the city to become an accountant. The details were incomplete, supplied by the proud and devoted Julian.

Crystal pursed her lips. Maybe she was being unreasonable. Was she jealous? Maybe she still had the hots for the now besotted one-woman-man Julian.

Crystal watched Mr and Mrs Clifton next door, hovering around outside supervising their grandchildren.

Crystal knew if she made a super effort she could still have Julian: for the occasional lunchtime romp, for example.

Mr Clifton wheeled the rubbish bins out to the pavement. Mrs Clifton rocked a baby in a pram back and forth.

But the thing was – was Crystal, at her age, prepared to put herself out there for the excitement of yet another futile romantic liaison? Probably not.

Mrs Clifton looked up, saw Crystal on the ladder and shook her head. She called out, 'Don't push your luck up there.'

Crystal waved good morning and said the weather had finally turned cold.

Mr Clifton said, 'Well, what do you expect for this time of the year?'

Crystal frowned. You can't please everyone all of the time.

*

A moonless night.

Two massive wild boars, their eyes ablaze, circle each other, fangs bared. Their mammoth razor-sharp horns either side of their heads vanquish the bush like scythes, stripping the trees, the grass and all of God's small creatures. The depth of their pupils expose unspeakable and immeasurable internal conflicts.

Outside, the icy wind from the mountains rattles the roof tiles and the leaf-laden gutters.

La Doctoresse forces her eyes to open. She reaches for the remote to turn the heater on. She has seen the Exit sign of her life, and is slowly backing towards it.

She must make some changes.

*

Next morning, Crystal opened her eyes and knew, without moving a muscle, that everything had changed during the night. The swish of traffic was the clue. A grey light crept round the corners of the blind. Crystal snapped the blind up to the top. Rain. Delicate silver shards of it, made opaque by the dark sky. Icy and shape-shifting on the road and between the leaves in the blocked gutters. Another world, with all that pollution washed away down the drains – including the dog poo hidden in the grassy verges which those slack dog owners had failed to scoop up with their plastic-covered fingers.

The huge magnolia tree next door was a sodden rotting mess.

The freshly washed linen strung across the clothes rack under the covered veranda beckoned Crystal to bring it inside. She banged on the wood of the French door frame, forcing the door to open and stepped outside onto the crunch of dead leaves.

There was Simon, wrapped in his mother's old mink coat, sitting on the tiles enveloping Crystal's daughter in animal fur as they joked around while feeding each other handfuls of popcorn, straight from the saucepan. Crystal wanted to remember this scene forever, her gorgeous blue-eyed daughter and her free-spirited lover.

She retrieved her cable-knit dressing-gown from the laundry basket, wrapped it around herself and hurried out to join them.

*

Still looking for Gypsy.

Gypsy snuggled up close to the Homeless Girl. Fuck, thought the Homeless Girl. I'm going to get drenched. The dog too. We'll both bloody well catch pneumonia.

*

Still looking for Gypsy.

An east coast low approached from the north.

Where was Gypsy? He'd be frightened by the approaching storm. Philip pushed himself up out of his chair and joined Rosemary at the window.

'It's good to see a bit of rain,' Rosemary said, thinking of the poor farmers and the drought and the losing of livelihoods.

'The garden will love it.'

Rosemary wanted to take the twins to Cooper Park to see the spectacle of the waterfall. 'Have you seen their gum boots?' she asked, thinking of how much fun they'd have running through the puddles. She'd ask Grace to come as well, but knew she'd say no. She preferred the company of her friends. Grace – out of nowhere sprang a happy vision of her determined and talented eldest child, self-satisfied and smiling, but now unreachable behind her bedroom door.

Rosemary resisted an impulse to run upstairs and shout through the door. She knew Grace was home. Had heard the click of the front door.

'Is that you, darling?' she had called, though it was way before the end of the school day, and had received a faint, 'Yes, it's me,' as the girl ran up the stairs two at a time to the retreat she'd made in the back room.

Grace's skill with the sewing machine and her remarkable portrait paintings made her mother's heart swell with pride.

Why had she withdrawn from her? What had she done wrong? Her birth in the year of the dragon so joyfully celebrated: her TV shows monitored – *Playschool, Dora the Explorer*: nothing too scary. The wooden letters that made up her name glued to her bedroom door, and as much television as she wanted because TV made her happy.

Rosemary zipped up her jacket and pulled on her gloves.

Philip was in the kitchen, boiling an egg.

Grace's tendencies towards feminism were taking on new radical undertones. Rosemary had found militant propaganda, including public protest leaflets, in Grace's room that morning (why shouldn't she snoop around – it was the only way she could find out what was going on); and on Grace's patchwork quilt she had seen a flyer advertising a consciousness-raising group to raise awareness of women's oppression. Beside it was a red poster with the words 'Get Angry and Smash Patriarchy'. And, on her new white melamine desk that Philip had assembled from Ikea, an unfinished essay argued for a move to radical political lesbianism.

That all-girl high school was the problem. They overdid the whole patriarchal society thing, and now the girls seemed to be anti-male. Rosemary knew Philip was very unhappy about what he saw as feminist politics being encouraged. And all because Rosemary had insisted Grace go to her old school: Girls Can Do Anything.

Rosemary wound a scarf around her neck. She'd walk to the park – always relaxing. The roads were slippery and dangerous. She'd have some thinking space without anyone asking questions.

'Mama. Mama.'

The twins were sitting on the bottom step, their boots and jackets on, ready to go. They both reached out to be picked up. She swung one on each hip, and they ambled off down the street.

Philip returned to the window. Bib and Bub those two boys with their matching knitted beanies, he thought. Philip knew Rosemary often wondered if she was a good enough mother. He couldn't understand why she'd think that. But he didn't think too deeply about most things. It was easier that way, although he delved into ancient Egypt, wanting to know what made the Egyptians strong enough to rule the world. He'd turned his research into a children's fiction series. As he spent most of his days in front of his computer, he had a stooped posture and pale face but, thanks to Rosemary, he ate healthily. Rosemary wasn't into historical fiction, though she admired the way he used history as his jumping-off point, entwining fact and fiction with plenty of forward momentum. But she didn't want to proofread his drafts. She tells people Philip would like nothing better than to have her spend her days sitting in a corner of his study listening to him read.

*

Kingston had come to regard the family photograph album as his inheritance. At the time his brother gave it to him, he didn't value the old pictures. He'd ripped them all out of the album, except the ones of himself and his brother.

Thinking to bury the pictures where they originated, he got in his car and drove to their old house. It had been totally demolished, and in its place stood two blocks of apartments.

*

The day had started off so well, with indulging in the buttery corn on the veranda and poached eggs and coffee for breakfast (Coco Pops and orange juice for Priscilla).

Simon had ground the coffee beans. The smell of the coffee percolating filled the sunroom. Simon looked so much in control – so together: eating, chatting, smiling, setting the table for breakfast, laying the cutlery out with a flourish – that Crystal had allowed herself to lean back on the leather couch with satisfaction.

The morning light picked up the subtleties of the colours of Simon's fur coat as he leaned over Crystal, gently securing her wispy curls behind her ears, raising her skirt and running his fingers along the inside of her soft thigh. Simon was about to slide his hand down Crystal's smooth, silky undies when they heard Priscilla approaching.

'I owe you one,' whispered Simon.

Crystal grinned at him and went to make another cup of coffee in the sunny kitchen.

After breakfast, they had walked down to the tennis courts at Cooper Park.

Simon had been to the Australian Open once. He'd often thought about how he enjoyed watching a hard-fought game of tennis. And here it was now, a version of it, being slogged out in front of him. And part of it all was Julian, playing doubles up on the top court by the children's playground. Simon focused his eyes. It was him all right, pelting those cross-court backhands to Dina as she sent the ball back at him into the far corner avoiding the person at the net.

Crystal laughed. The caffeine hit from the second cup of coffee charged through her veins. The park, the courts, the playground and the path up through the gully stretched before her. She felt like Dorothy in the *Wizard of Oz* standing at the crossroads. The drip from her cold nose kept distracting her. All she wanted to think about was getting Priscilla into bed early and snogging on the couch with Simon. But, as usual, that's not the way things turned out.

The trouble started when they were out the back throwing the ball through the basketball hoop. Priscilla, annoyed because she had difficulty getting the ball high enough to score goals, stormed inside, slamming the back door behind her. Once in the house, she grabbed a packet of Tiny Teddies that Granny had given her, opened the front door, un-latched the front gate and hurried off to the Homeless Girl's cave.

Simon kicked the basketball on to the roof. He didn't want to play any more either. Crystal picked up the ball when it rolled back down the roof tiles. Simon grabbed it from her. He kicked it in her direction. It struck her in the leg, causing a cry of alarm. Crystal hugged herself with her arms. From a crouched position, she told Simon that he should learn to control his impulses.

'I wish I could.'

And that was an honest statement. There are other things too, but he knows not to put them into words: that he feels disconnected from, and has no optimism for, the world. He is filled with anxiety. He cannot get away from his own pessimism. It's depressing, but these are the facts.

*

All human beings are fatally flawed.

Who had said that? His dad? His brother? The Bible? Or the man at the back of the bus on the way to school who would expose his flaccid member and give it a jig? Whoever had said it, Kingston was sure it ap-plied to himself as he grew into adolescence, overweight and pimple-ridden. Why wasn't he like everyone else? Because his dad was behind bars? It was true he spent his afternoons in his room trying to glimpse the teenage girl who lived next door through the venetian blinds, or the other teenage girl in the house up the back when she'd play in her backyard. The family next door had invited him to go swimming with them to the beach once, but his mother said no. Sharks, she said. You don't want to be in the ocean at dusk.

Every day, as the afternoon darkened into night, Kingston had watched the family next door through the slats of the venetian blinds. The dad, the mum, the two kids – he could see them all in his mind, together on the couch or around the dinner table.

*

Still looking for Gypsy.

Priscilla rattles a handful of coins near the Homeless Girl's ear. Will it be enough to buy a Coke?

She shoves a Tiny Teddy between the teenager's pale lips. The poor lost girl opens the puffy lids of her spaced-out eyes.

'Wake up. Wake up,' Priscilla begs, though she is not sure why she feels so desperate.

A blurry picture appears on the scarred surface of the Homeless Girl's brain. She has a thought but then it disappears. She closes her eyes. Priscilla's tears splosh distraught and moist onto her cheeks and add warmth to their icy surface.

The Homeless Girl sighs faintly, reaches for the child's wrist, encircles it in a tight grasp as she tries to remember what she had been planning. Oh yes, that was it. Money for a Coke. A Coke will help. This child is turning out to be useful.

She eats the packet of Tiny Teddies and falls back into an exhausted sleep beside the golden Labrador.

The dog wags his tail at Priscilla, who is happy that there is someone to watch over the poor lost girl. She gives him a pat then tiptoes away.

Priscilla treasures the Homeless Girl – whether or not she's actually her runaway sister. She would do anything to help her. But she loves her mother too and doesn't want to cause worry. She must get home.

Soon the bitter wind will wake the homeless teenager. The inescapable relentlessness of the cold will erase all memory of grabbing money from the child. But now the winter solstice has passed, the days will lighten and brighten and she'll start to feel better. And more possibilities will occur to her.

*

Simon had spent the summer of his thirty-first year at a hairdressing salon in the suburbs. It had been a time of demanding work but personal loss and, when he had left there, he'd found himself with enough cash to buy a chair and rent a space in a salon nearby. He bought black leather with chrome trim.

He'd cut and moulded hair in that new place in a crazy-mixed-up state of mind. Every morning, he'd driven to work sobbing, grieving for the wife and son he'd left behind in France.

The idea of dying had crossed his mind, but he'd never attempted to act on it.

He'd kept his head down at work and listened with empathy to the stories his clients disclosed to him.

*

Jean-Claude. Twenty-two years old. From Paris, France. Jean-Claude kneels on the floor in front of her where she reclines on the flower-patterned cushions of the wicker couch. He's determined to remove her pantyhose.

La Doctoresse lets him take them off, regretting already she said her former student could come home with her, and for saying he could spend the night on her couch after he'd missed the train back to Paris.

And then, just as her underpants slide down to her ankles and over her feet, she realises she's wearing those old daggy to-the-waist undies which she should have replaced long ago, jarring her delicate sensibilities and bringing her straight back to reality.

She moves away from him and leans back, wondering at her own stupidity, as she grabs the pantyhose and the undies and stuffs them behind one of the bright cushions.

She stares at him and realises that not only has she done something unethical, she has allowed herself to be led down a dead-end again.

'Does this mean you're my girlfriend now?' he whispers.

She shoves him off her.

'I promise I'll stay on the couch. You know I didn't want to wait for hours for another train. I promise I'll be a gentleman.'

She seems to have switched off and sits quietly. She's heard a car door slam. It can't be Lawrence already, can it? He said he wouldn't be home till really late.

'You have to go.'

'Not now,' he pleads. 'Don't kick me out on the street after driving me back to your place and having your way with me.' He kisses her neck, leans against her until she falls back. He's on all fours, like a dog on heat.

'It's my son. I don't know when he'll be home.' She sees her own reflection in the metal blades of the overhead fan; her flushed face and sparkling eyes. She pulls at the lace hem of her skirt. She composes herself, fumbles under the cushions for her underpants and pantyhose.

He cries out in complaint, flattens her with his body, hitches up her skirt and eases himself in. They rock back and forth on the couch like two crazy children playing at seesaw.

'A few minutes,' he begs. 'Just a few minutes more.'

The back door clicks open. They spring apart.

'See. I told you,' she snaps. 'That he could come back at any time.'

'It's okay,' he calms her. 'The light is on. And we're just sitting here on the couch talking.'

All the same, she jumps up. She smooths her skirt down. She'd like to say something to him – that this has all been a dreadful mistake, that she shouldn't have said she'd give him a lift from the party.

But she liked the way he danced.

She should have said, 'Go home and find someone your own age.'

Her spunkiest ex-student zips himself up. He thinks he will go home. He thinks he will wait on the freezing platform at Nice, get approached by a pervert, attacked by a gang of skinheads, the thin streak of a bloke that he is.

In time, what happens is he goes to a dance at his local bar, meets a girl, kisses her afterwards on the street and eventually gets invited to move into her studio apartment on the left bank.

*

Twelve years old and unable to bear another day of school, Kingston had jumped the school fence, heart pounding in fear because he knew, if found out, the punishment would be swift and brutal, especially when they told his mother, she who had worked her butt off to send him to this school. But, at that moment, he felt it was a matter of life or death, or taking a stand, or something like that because he couldn't tolerate being told what to do another moment. He'd run down the hill, ducked behind a power pole while the sun beat down on his straw boater. His courage almost left him when he saw two school prefects marching up towards him. If he was put on daily detention, he'd be forced to do more Latin homework. The thing was, he'd always be an outsider at school; even if he wrote the answers on his ruler and on the inside of his wrist, he'd still be hopeless at exams. He couldn't keep his mind inside the classroom, and it would never change, unless he had brain surgery.

As luck would have it, one of the prefects called out to him, 'Watch how you present yourself in school uniform, boy. Tuck yourself in. Button up your blazer.'

And that was it. He was in the clear for once.

*

'My grandmother said to me, "You'll find in life that it's a man's world."'

'A grandmother?'

'That's right.'

'You've never mentioned a grandmother.'

Crystal, who was circumspect about her family history, reddened.

'Sticks and stones will break your bones, but names will never hurt you,' chanted Priscilla.

'That's enough,' said Crystal and Simon at the same time.

Crystal grinned. Simon grinned back. You never know, thought Crystal, maybe things will turn out all right in the end. Maybe what we should do is spend some quality time, just the two of us, Simon and me. Crystal did her best to think of things they both enjoyed and could do together. A train trip to Cabramatta to look at the shops and a Vietnamese lunch? She'd be the one picking up the bill, so why not make a selfish choice?

'Listen to this,' enthused Simon. '"A man may be born, but in order to be born he must first die, and in order to die he must first awake. A man will renounce any pleasures you like but he will not give up his suffering".'

'Where did that come from?'

'There was a pile of them in a box in the attic.'

Crystal thought she'd got rid of everything that related to Kingston. So much for that.

'I don't intend to give up on life's pleasures. Call me a hedonist if you like, but I'm not one for suffering, except when it's forced on me.'

'I think there's more to suffering than meets the eye,' said Simon, examining the intricate decoration on a golden Balinese cremation tower.

'You could be right,' said Crystal and went on wiping down the kitchen bench tops.

Priscilla went on colouring in her *Mindfulness* book. 'From dust to dust,' she chanted in a sing-song voice.

The cat jumped on Simon's lap and dug her claws into his jeans.

'Ouch,' Simon yelped and shoved the cat off. 'This cat needs her claws clipped.'

'Mm. Maybe,' said Crystal, looking up from unstacking the dishwasher. She dried her hands on her apron and gave Simon's broad shoulders a hug.

*

It had been a cold morning. Hard to drag herself out of bed and Kingston was at school, so his mother had made herself a warm shower and stood under it thinking about all the people rushing off to work, lined up in their cars outside the window, their impatient horns blaring. She listened to the sounds of life after retrenchment. Not working was lonely – so she kept telling Kingston – too bloody quiet, with no job to go to.

Mrs Patterson had closed her eyes and let her mind loosen and float, down to the green gully of the park. She could see the sun on the leaves of the trees that ringed the tennis courts, trees she'd never forgotten nor knew the names of, but occasionally brought to mind to calm herself. Her little piece of heaven in school holidays. A sanctuary to play in, she'd thought, is a child's birthright. She'd hoped Kingston had had a safe place to go to, but she knew otherwise. What chance did he have with a father repeatedly in trouble with the law?

She'd hoped he'd made friends at the new school. She was sure he had and that made her happy. Thinking vaguely of partnerships and choices in life, she'd dried herself quickly before stroking cream onto her body, rubbing firmly down her legs, and that's when she'd felt it. A lump. Well, more a protrusion in the groin.

Mrs Patterson decided it was a hernia. In hospital they did the usual tests before operating. In the end, it turned out there was disease in her pancreas. During a short period of remission, Kingston's mother travelled to Hawaii with her sons before coming home to die.

*

Still looking for Gypsy.

Those men from Woollahra Council whose job it was to get rid of abandoned cars from Cooper Park had discovered the Homeless Girl and Gypsy snuggled together.

'You've got your whole life in front of you. Stay off the drugs.' So the psychotherapist and nurses up at the clinic told Amelie, which is what the Homeless Girl had said her name was.

The corrective order included placement in a foster home, regular drug testing, mental health counselling and monitoring of Amelie's progress in finding employment.

Gypsy stayed at the vet's until Amelie was well enough to collect him. They'd had enough of him at the surgery chewing everyone's shoes and raiding the storeroom to eat the boxes of cat food, cardboard and all.

When the time came, the psychotherapist drove Amelie to the vet's to pick up Gypsy, and then drove them to the foster home he'd been able to locate that would take them both in. An elderly Scottish couple.

*

Simon closes the front door with a gentle click. It feels good to be out in the morning air of Lake Derwent after the smell of the big breakfast fry-up in the B&B. The rain has increased in intensity and the trees are bending with the weight of it. No birds are visible on the boughs. The newsagent has delivered the papers but, at the fire station, a siren whines. He pulls the hood of his parka over his head and steps across the water that gushes down the gutters up the steep hill – south – across a bridge and over the railway line. A train disappears into a tunnel.

He stops at the pedestrian crossing in front of the school, the rain bouncing on his hood as children amble across the playground to their classrooms. He would like to call out to them, to tell them to hurry out of the rain but he walks on up to the next set of traffic lights. Past the chicken shop, avoiding puddles in the bitumen, waiting as the siren blares closer then speeds past.

As soon as he inserts his key in the lock of the hire car, he knows he cannot drive today. He turns back down the road, over the bridge and past Coleridge's house and heads out towards the beautiful lake.

Maybe he'll find inspiration in the early morning dark. He'll stay for as long as it takes. For a moment, Simon feels an opening to possibility and then the thought flashes out of his mind. He passes the barred windows of the antique jewellery shop, then the Italian clothing boutique, and crosses the road. There's no pavement now, just the green grass, a mush of sodden earth under his feet. There are muddy pools in places and he tells himself he doesn't really know where he is going. After a kilometre, he can hear, behind him, the comforting sound of the waterfall.

The Lakes Poet School, or Bards of the Lake, were initially derogatory names: the school of whining and hypochondriacal poets that haunt the Lakes. For William Wordsworth, who lived there after many years of wandering, the Lakes became bound up with his identity as a poet.

*

'Are those shoes Sketchers?' asked the large-but-toned woman with the tiny braided plaits who seemed to live in the reception foyer at the gym (sometimes napping in a chair).

Simon nodded, then sighed heavily. Hardly time to fit in a gym workout these days. But he loved his lightweight perfect-for-travelling Sketchers sport shoes, although travel wouldn't be happening again any time soon. Crystal had started a new job and wouldn't be entitled to holidays for a very long time.

Where is Priscilla? She was here a moment ago.

Simon stepped over a large-but-toned woman's gym bag and looked out the door. No sign of Priscilla out on the road. But there are Dina and Julian (without clothing racks this time) lumbering down the street under a pile of For Women with Curves boxes.

'They shouldn't let all these people come in for free at weekends,' the large-but-toned woman with the tiny braided plaits whined. 'I don't care if it's a special promotion. It's not fair on members, even if they can bring a friend for free. The yoga class had been so packed there was hardly a spot left to put your mat down.' She looked over at the trestle table now being set up by Julian and the boxes of For Women with Curves active wear on the floor.

Dina had permission from the club manager to erect a pop up shop. She plugged in the steam presser to give the clothes a quick once-over before they went on display.

Dina's target market closed her eyes. Dina cajoled her to get out of the chair and have a look at the sportswear. Everything was out on the table now in neat colour-coordinated groups. Simon retreated towards the men's room, wanting to make an escape before they noticed him.

The large-but-toned woman grunted as she hoisted herself up. 'What am I doing here?' she asked.

'You just did a yoga class by the looks of it,' said Dina.

Simon peered into the ladies' change room. Where is Priscilla?

Julian called out, 'Simon. Don't you remember me? You and I were in the back row in all those rugby photos. We'd have a laugh when you made those funny faces.'

'Are those shoes Sketchers?' asked the forgetful large-but-toned woman pointing at Simon's shoes.

'Yes,' said Dina. 'Sketchers are great. I've got a pair of their walking shoes too.'

'It's not fair,' complained the large woman. 'They don't make them wide enough for my bunion feet.'

'The thing is,' said Julian, 'nothing in life is fair. The rich get richer and the poor get poorer.'

Simon screwed up his face. Was this an involuntary tic? The old schooldays were a distant memory. There was very little he could bring to mind.

Dina moved in closer and peered into Simon's eyes. Dina wanted Simon to know that she, Dina, held him to blame for Crystal's lack of regular attendance at the For Women With Curves pyramid-selling workshops and for Crystal's inability to see the difference between what she wanted to do in life and what she had to do: the difference between activities she found nurturing, and those that left her feeling depleted.

In order to make a stronger point on the issue, she repositioned herself in front of the Fuel Zone refrigerated cabinet and lunged forward into a Warrior Woman pose. She lined up her gaze over an outstretched arm to beyond the middle finger of her front hand.

Simon thought she looked amazing. He felt the stirring in his trackies he usually felt when a woman spoke with such authority. Simon was so annoyed with himself that he couldn't concentrate on the point she was making.

What he did understand her to say was that he and Crystal were living a safe traditional suburban life similar to the old sitcoms like *Leave It To Beaver*. They'd settled into a domestic rut with no surprises. Dina said she'd bring over a set of *Housewives in the City* to inspire Crystal to action.

Simon covered his ears. He didn't have to listen to this crap.

And he didn't, as things turned out, because that was when, heated by the air from the steam presser, the fire alarm went off. Water gushed down from the ceiling as Julian reached over to turn off the power. A shout, sparks and then silence.

Simon made use of this change in focus and headed out the door. He'd come back another time for his gym bag and yoga mat. He was sure reception would keep them safe behind the front desk in the lost property box.

*

Priscilla searched around the tennis courts. No abandoned cars. And no one in the ladies toilets. Where was the Homeless Girl? Was she like all those big girls who did a runner on their little sisters? Priscilla couldn't work it out. All she knew was she had a funny feeling in her belly.

*

Julian and Dina had a long chat about Simon while they sipped their after-dinner brandies. They exchanged gossip about his poor history with women and his lack of ability to be satisfied with whoever he was with. Julian had more gossip to tell than Dina, though Dina was interested in the European psyche because that's where her favourite movies were made and shown at Palace cinemas, just up the road from where they lived.

After that, Dina had some invoices to send out and sent them. Julian couldn't settle down to writing a new post for their Women with Curves blog site, so he decided to send an email to Crystal instead. After all, she'd been his childhood sweetheart. In it was all sorts of information that Crystal should be made aware of. Julian felt guilt rippling down from his chest to his stomach, but, what the heck, it was for her own good.

*

Still looking for Gypsy.

Rosemary hadn't seen Simon for a long time. Maybe it was all for the best. She brought to mind her husband's sad, deeply sensitive, transparent blue eyes. He'd guessed right about the dog too. That he was lost to them. Probably found a home he liked better. And Philip was getting plenty of offers for lecturing modules at the university. Life was pretty good, all things considered. Except for Grace. What had gone wrong? She used to adore him. And now she seemed to be avoiding both of them. She hardly gave her little twin brothers the time of day either.

All she wanted to do was hang out with Marta. They were in high school together. Kindred spirits. Apparently, Marta had gone to Grace's home that morning before school and they'd fiddled around with make-up for a while and had no trouble coming up with the money needed for a new eye make-up kit plus the train fare into the QVB to buy it. Marta intended saving hers for the weekend. Not so Grace. By the time they were sitting on the bus headed for school, she'd painted around her eyes and added glitter to her eyelids.

They jumped off the bus at Chatswood Station, skateboards tucked under their arms. Grace led the way.

Marta followed the bright green and yellow of Grace's board down the ramp. Grace was a jock, everyone said: a determination to win.

'Make marriage equality a reality,' she'd found time to yell out as, jumping clear of the skateboard at the bottom of the ramp, it had crashed into the glass wall of the chemist shop. She grabbed the board, jumped back on, and the two girls disappeared down the mall, skating as fast as they could. At the traffic lights at the end of the mall, they skated across without looking.

A scream, then silence.

*

Mrs Patterson lay back on the freshly laundered white pillows that Kingston had plumped up behind her. Kingston checked she was comfortable before edging toward the bedroom door.

Kingston had had to get special permission from the school to stay at home. They had been very compassionate and said they'd organise a private tutor for him. They didn't know he preferred carer duties to the rough and tumble of school life.

'What sort of cake would you like me to bake today?'

She grunted. She wasn't interested in food. Everything made her nauseous. She'd lost most of her hair and had shrunk to skeleton proportions.

He worked away in the kitchen before returning to the bedroom with a carrot cake on a platter and a cup of tea.

'Too milky, too milky,' his mother shouted, tea spilling from her cup, sighing for her good health, which she had taken for granted. Oh, to be young and healthy and not bedridden. She whipped herself into a frenzy of self-pity 'It's not fair! It's not fair!' she cried.

By the time the tea had been drunk, the cake lay on the plate in ruins.

He carried the tray back downstairs, where he sat in the kitchen, totally silent. He was not aware of time passing. Instead, he looked back to other times when silence had been the norm. When, after school, he'd stood at the window of his bedroom listening for the sound of his mother's car. When, silently, he had watched his brother Clark pack his bag for the last time. And if he heard sounds, it was his mother shouting at Clark, 'Idiot. Idiot. Just like your father. You'll never amount to anything.'

I believe that one defines oneself by reinvention. To not be like your parents. To not be like your friends. To be yourself. To cut yourself out of stone. Who was it who said that? He'd seen it on the net somewhere. Someone who'd also had a cruel and bitter mother, or perhaps someone whose father was also locked away in prison. Kingston was hopeless at remembering who said what to whom. He felt a failure as a son, but had always done his best. But that, of course, wasn't good enough. He hadn't even been beside her holding her hand the night she died in the hospital. He'd been in front of the television at home catching up on old episodes of Homer Simpson.

*

One morning in the south of France, when the sun rose warmly, high and transformative, in that shape-shifting way that it can turn the ragged clouds into smoke signals, and he'd been driving since sunrise with the assistance of caffeine – well, and whatever else he'd popped in his mouth – and without turning away from the Grande Corniche, he'd switched stations and dramatic pulsating music filled the car: the incorporation of jazz and classical music from Piazolla's *Nuevo* tango. His solar plexus had radiated warmth like the sun with understanding and exhaustion, and a long-standing and lonesome wish that, if only Sarah were here to share it, they could dance the tango and everything would be all right.

So he'd stopped by the side of the road, opened his laptop and logged on to Skype.

Sarah had accepted his call. Lawrence, she said, was safe asleep.

Safe from Simon. His inconsistency, unreliability and flakiness. His forgetfulness regarding important dates: like grand finals and school prize-giving days.

'Simon,' she said, 'leave us alone. Nothing has changed.' She told him that she was waiting to close down the laptop and go to bed.

He remembered how her neck used to ache from too much time at her computer. His massaging of her shoulders didn't help.

Simon could see the moonlight spilling through the panelled windows of the top-floor art deco apartment, saw the view all the way across to Saint Jean Cap Ferrat which must have cost the earth.

Was Lawrence there, the sound of footsteps – was that him or the heavy-footed guy from downstairs?

And then, pushing back from her desk to show him his time was up, 'Fidelity is boring. Remember?'

Everyone deserves a second chance. Doesn't he?

The telephone icon on the screen turned red. Skype had been disconnected.

He fought back anger. What about forgiveness? Don't they teach those things at church any more?

A taste of his insides rising into his throat signified he needed to learn to suck it up. He opened the car door and it landed like yellow custard on the grass verge and speckled his pale grey canvas rubber-soled shoes. He avoided his guts and stepped out of the car.

When he'd cleaned up, he drove slowly away because, whether you are experiencing loss, self-hatred or any other powerful emotion, you process it quicker if you give it plenty of space.

Still looking for Gypsy.

He sat in his car just after dawn watching Rosemary's windows until a light went on. It was still early when he turned the key in the ignition, started the car and headed for home.

Had Simon watched a bit longer, he might have heard Rosemary's mobile ring, would definitely have seen her blinds snap up, would even maybe have heard the cry that plummeted to the pavement to lie like an injured bird spotlighted by the morning sky.

But instead he hurried home, thinking mostly of Crystal while the sun took its time to creep up until it dominated the sky, bright and shiny-like-a-button on the developing day, somewhere to the left of the ridge of Cooper Park. Another day. Another opportunity. Simon vowed to be more grateful.

*

As she did every Saturday at five-thirty p.m., Crystal rang her father in Coffs Harbour.

Sure, he'd be delighted to have Priscilla for a few days provided she promised not to take off on her own again without telling anyone.

Crystal put her on the bus, praying to an unknown goddess that she would stay on the bus till it reached Coffs.

She needn't have doubted her daughter's word. She loved to stay with Poppy. In particular, she adored sitting on the tractor in front of him and doing the steering. She loved helping Poppy with all his maintenance jobs inside and outside the house. She also enjoyed going with him on his fishing trips and having a go at rowing his small boat that was padlocked to a tree in a tiny bay down the end of the street.

The best part, though, despite all the fish they caught and sold to the fish shop, was coming back at the end of the day, when she'd pull out the daily newspaper from the letter box and race into the house.

She'd locate one of Poppy's special pencils and a rubber and turn to the crosswords at the back. Poppy would lumber in, saying, 'Time to do the puzzles before a game of Chinese Chequers.'

Later, she'd go up the stairs to sleep in Mummy's old bunk bed, although Poppy had turned the room into a library/bedroom. The shelves were covered with books – an antique fishing rod hung on one wall. Priscilla loved looking through the medical textbooks in particular. She'd always wanted to know how things worked, especially the brain. 'I want to be a brain surgeon when I grow up,' she liked to say when people would ask. 'I want to look inside people's heads and see how it all works.'

One night in this room, Priscilla dreamed a very scary dream of the Homeless Girl stabbed with needles, like a voodoo doll. Her grandfather found her hiding under the doona on the top bunk, pressed against the wall. And, outside, the cloud-filled pale sky did its best to beam on the rustling fronds of the palm trees.

'But there are no homeless children in Sydney – unless they want to be homeless. Didn't Mummy tell you that?'

'Mummy doesn't know the Homeless Girl.'

*

Marta had skated on ahead so fast that next day she'd found she had pulled a muscle in her calf, though at the time she hadn't felt anything, nothing but scared as she'd scooted off like a reincarnated Frida Kahlo with her mono brow forehead, denim jacket, flowered shorts, legs pale and lightly covered with hair rigid above her platform sandals that helped propel her along the pavement in escape all the way back to the all-girl high school, where she and Grace were enrolled, which turned out to be a longer scoot than she realised.

And having found her favourite teacher, she'd blubbered out the sequence of events, her head buried in his shoulder. His bewildered hands had wiped away her tears and he'd wondered, 'I thought they built girls much tougher these days.' He'd recommended she keep all the details of the crash and its aftermath to herself. And she had. She'd been to the hospital a few times, although she managed to avoid Grace's parents. What could she say to them?

As the school year continued and no one called on Marta as a witness, she imagined that fate had let her off scot-free.

*

The lips pursed: those golden lips on the gold-painted Buddha that reclined on top of the microwave. They exhaled a kiss.

Kingston steadied himself against the bench top. He was aware that drinking all that water and eating all those green leafy vegetables they fed you at Beverly Springs Wellness Centre was affecting his equilibrium. He knew that if you drank too much water, it could affect the salt levels in your brain. It's not as if he was forced to stay here – not as if he'd been locked up and the key thrown away. He'd get his balance back before deciding what to do next. Something, or someone, would present itself, or herself.

Maybe he'd get to see Madam Betty again on one of those group walks when they'd all pile into the minivan and drive into a national park.

He stroked the fur of his chest, remembering her strong hands on his body. Kingston moistened his lips with his tongue. The gorgeous Madam Betty – finally a masseuse who could loosen the tension in his neck. He always got a rise if someone spent that much time with their hands on his body. But here? Where was he exactly?

This is where he'd hibernate during the dark winter days and nights. But he didn't belong. It wasn't his 'tribe'. It's not as if anyone really understood his situation.

*

Crystal and Simon went by train to the Southern Highlands. They stayed at a hotel on the railway line.

'Priscilla would love the trains,' said Crystal, sitting outside the Bicycle Café in the chilly air sipping hot soup, her hand resting with propriety on Simon's thigh.

'She wouldn't want to be woken up with their whistling and rumblings,' said Simon.

For Simon, it all came down to this: a freezing room in an old art deco hotel, the cold July night closing in on them, keeping them together in front of an open fire, where the only thing possible to say was 'I adore you. I want to spend the rest of my life with you. Let's tie the knot.' But Simon hadn't said this, and then the ongoing interruption of the phone and the excited exclaiming of her daughter's name as Crystal rummaged in her handbag's large mouth. Simon looked out through the steel bars of the window, his irritation only noticeable by the had-enough twitching of his right eyelid. He wanted to scream, 'I exist! Here I am!'

*

Rosemary prayed for a miracle to restore her smashed and broken girl.

She met with Dr Watt in his surgery, perched like an eyrie on the tenth floor of a new building, made of glass and steel. When she was shown in to his rooms, she was dazzled by a blaze of early-spring sunlight falling down the sheets of floor-to-ceiling glass. He'd invited her to sit but Rosemary could not tolerate the thought of settling herself on a chair.

She went instead and stood at the glass wall, high above the park. Directly below her there was a frangipani tree, the spring greening of its branches just beginning, not covered yet with summer's perfume. Dr Watt sat at his desk scrolling through the files on his computer while speaking into his mobile. The purple cover of the phone made her think of finding her new smartphone with its purple casing in the letter box that morning and feeling the soft malleable texture of the gel and the unexpected smell of rubber. How her mind wandered, even on the most focused of occasions.

She turned from the glass; the outside had become intolerable now. 'Well, doctor,' she said, a little too shrill, putting on the bright, forced tone of a first-year kindergarten teacher, 'will she ever walk again?'

The room was still.

'Too early to tell.'

'Grace,' she said to herself softly. 'Oh Grace, my little princess.'

A plane crossed the sky. At any moment, Rosemary thought, the plane will plummet, it will plummet. But it didn't. A small boy on a scooter wavered along the path beside the creek that cut through the park, past the slippery dip and swings in the children's play area, the ranger's truck piled high with weeds, the man-made caves, the sunny café, the six tennis courts with their tightly strung nets. In a minute, he will topple off his scooter, he will topple over into the murky water. But he didn't.

She was aware she was weeping. Dr Watt pushed a packet of tissues across the table in her direction. She blew her nose.

She walked out into the day as if she was stepping out in a different country, one where no one was visible on the street but her.

Car roofs glimmered. An older man in a linen suit was walking away slowly across the parking area. Even at that distance, she imagined she could hear his canvas shoes shuffling carefully on the pavement.

Her thoughts spiralled. Who can she talk to? Who is prepared to listen to her? Not Philip. He blamed her because she'd encouraged the girl to use the skateboard as a means of transport. His pain would not allow more complex accusations to add to his grieving.

Philip had been visiting his brother in Leura when it happened. And the partner of the same brother had travelled by train all the way to Sydney to deliver a pot of chicken soup to their doorstep.

More food drops had been left at their house since. Her mother arrived at the weekend. His own mother would be joyously welcomed in this time of great need but she lay next to his father in a steel box in a brick wall at La Perouse. And, anyway, his parents would have found a way to make the accident his fault.

*

The Southern Highlands had regenerated Crystal. Since coming back, she'd given a lot of thought to working a second job on her day off. She'd been thinking about it for some time, ever since the split with Kingston. With some extra money coming in, things would be less stressful. Wasn't that the aim of life, to hang loose and enjoy it? A second job would provide the money for her to turn the under-the-house playroom (the room that no one used) into a studio apartment, to bring in more cash. Crystal lay back, her dreamy eyes glazing over with joy as she smiled to herself, imagining how things might unfold. A regular extra weekly income from a studio could change her life. She began to flick through *Bathroom and Kitchen* magazines looking for tiny-house designs.

Crystal pestered Simon into carting that pile of personally-signed-by-the-greats footballs in the bedroom down to the playroom underneath the house. She told Simon he could be more assertive, make some other kind of contact with his son apart from footballs posted from the other side of the world.

Simon thought, as he bundled the footballs into a box, that he should try and bring in more money too. His hairdressing clientele numbers had stagnated, although the women seemed to love him. How do you grow a business? Aren't personal recommendations the best advertisement? Simon was forty-four years old but lacked the self-discipline and determination required to be a successful businessman.

He sat in the bright sun on the outside stairs that led to the playroom. One of those huge lizards lived down there. He could hear one slithering into the foliage. The lizard discreetly made its way to the front door and slipped in before the door closed behind it. Oh no. Now

Simon was locked out. Where was the spare key? Not Blu-tacked to the underside of the window ledge where Crystal usually left it. He was shut out of the house and needed to wait for Crystal to come home and let him in. He'd have a game of mini pool in the playroom.

At three in the afternoon, Julian had rung on the landline. He'd wanted to speak to Crystal about something or other. Had Julian known Simon could hear the phone ringing above his head down in the playroom but was unable to get back in to the house, he wouldn't have thought that to be unusual. The spare rooms and playrooms in many neighbourhoods are infested with men like Simon who've found themselves banished to the doghouse, or other confined spaces.

*

Still looking for Gypsy.

At first in the early days, they'd waited still incredulous, and Philip had stood by the window wiping his eyes, staring into space and mumbling to himself. Rosemary had not been able to get through to him by declarative statements, cajoling, nor hugs or hand squeezing either, and her worrying thoughts had had to be suppressed. Then her mind had turned to Simon.

And once, when they'd been asked to wait outside while a nurse changed the dressings and Philip had sat stony-faced in the noisy reception area, a newspaper unopened under his arm, his unseeing glance no glance at all but just another way to acknowledge her invisibility, then, just that once, she'd driven down to Cooper Park to the Friday night tennis game but Simon wasn't there. Where was he? She wanted to tell him what had happened. She'd even barged in to the men's toilets looking for him. Distress was sending her around the twist, a fifty-year-old wailing banshee unable to control her emotions.

*

'That's life. It's what happens to you while you're making other plans, just like John Lennon said. Crazy things happen all the time. We deal with them and take pleasure in helping others.'

Enough, Hermione, thought Philip. Enough of your glass half-full jargon. 'Yes, Grace stopped speaking straight after the accident, you know that. No, I don't want to throw the runes to find out if she'll ever speak or walk again. No, I don't want to ask another question.'

Hermione reached into the pouch of rune stones, closed her eyes and concentrated before taking a rune from the bag.

'You're wasting your time,' Philip yelled at her. 'You can't make her speak. You've had your chance.'

Did he say that? Had he given up hope? The thing was, he'd had enough of Hermione and her weird ways.

Hermione looked down at the stone. '*Teiwaz*. English name, Warrior. *Teiwaz* is the rune of courage, dedication and absolute trust in one's own resources. Look within yourself and deeply analyse the foundations of your life.'

'There's nothing magical about the runes. You can stop now. I know we all need to connect to our intuition.'

Grace lay there on the bed, her eyes closed. Her body rigid. She'd pulled the sheet up to just below her nose.

Philip looked away from the super-intuitive Hermione to pat Grace's hand. She made a whimpering sound. Panic tightened his chest. It was like that time he was out on the golf course and thought he was about to be struck by lightning. He'd heard a lightning bolt followed by a clap of thunder and knew what could happen next: a lightning strike. He'd thrown his club down and run for cover.

Grace's eyes were squeezed shut. Brown fluid drained through a tube from under the bed sheet and down into a small collection bag.

'Sweetie pie,' cajoled Hermione. 'Open your eyes. Look at your father.'

Philip glared at Hermione. He clenched his hand into his pocket so he wouldn't use it to slap her across the face.

'Self-control,' intuited Hermione.

'I'll lose it if you don't stop this charade. Take your stones and coins and get out of here.'

'Come on, take it easy.'

'You take it easy. Please go.'

Philip had first met Hermione in the hospital cafeteria. She specialised in healing the sick by interpreting omens from the gods using methods that many called a load of hocus-pocus. Hermione had offered to help. But the casting of the rune stones, the shaking and tossing of I Ching coins, the figuring out of numerical values of the heads and tails, the adding up, the collection, the tossing of the coins another five times. And for what? It made no difference. The girl still refused to speak.

Now Hermione stiffened. She crossed to Grace and took hold of her wrist. She picked up the girl's cold hand gently and pressed it to her lips. 'Speak up,' she said, and drew in a deep breath. 'You're a gorgeous young woman,' she said. 'You've got your whole life ahead of you.' She walked to the door leaving Grace, Philip and the room behind her.

*

'Is there a smart TV in this place?' asked Kingston.

'Of course there is, Kingston,' said Madam Betty. 'Netflix, Stan, Presto. Streaming. We've got it all.'

'So many people don't realise what they're missing out on.'

'Not me. I watch an episode of something or other every night. There's a TV room, you know. You just have to make a reservation on the whiteboard outside the dining room for whatever time you want.'

*

La Doctoresse de Anti-ageing, her face still covered in perspiration from the cycling, turned off the Basse Corniche above Nice and into the health food store parking area. She rode over to the bicycle rack, locked up her black and flamingo-pink carbon fibre Trek Silque SL, tried to release the choking straps of her helmet, but her fingers resisted.

She stood astride her bike facing the Super Marche blackboard, reading the list of daily specials, telling herself to snap out of it.

She'd promised Lawrence she'd pick up some chocolate on her way home from her ride. He preferred milk chocolate, but because they didn't have a fresh vegetable in the house, or a piece of fruit, she'd stopped off here at the organic supermarket.

She was exhausted. She'd first have a quick coffee before facing the shopping and all the decisions she'd need to make.

She was fed up with herself. She knew there were plenty of other people out there on the road who were hauling the baggage of failed marriages. The thing was, what she couldn't get out of her mind was her son. What does it mean for a child when his mother's best present is the destruction of her marriage to his father? She must let it go.

Simon had loved preparing the Christmas meal for *la Doctoresse* when they'd lived here near her work at the Healthy Ageing Clinic. Simon used to laugh about her patients, referring to them as the worried wealthy who wanted to stay young.

Sarah looked at her mobile: a present from *le Professeur of Nutrition* (he'd typed his telephone number in). He didn't give presents to all the academics, scientific researchers and practitioners at the Anti-ageing Medicine World Congress 'promoting Science for tomorrow' in Monaco. He seemed to have taken a special liking to her.

An aproned waiter balanced a half cup of black coffee, a jug of hot milk and a glass of water on his arm. He laid them out on the small round table in front of her.

'*Merci*,' she said. '*Merci a toi.*'

She'd apologised to him for her poor level of French when he'd greeted her in English. He knew she wasn't able to exchange more than the basic level of pleasantries.

Last time, he'd held up a glass and a jug to point out the difference between asking for a carafe of water and a glass. 'Green is *vert*, right?' he said.

She nodded.

'A glass is *verre*, like green, but different.'

'*Oui.*'

He'd pulled out a piece of paper from behind the counter and written in big block letters: *VERT* = GREEN; *VERRE* = GLASS; *UN VERRE D'EAU*. When she'd been able to order a glass of water in French, he'd punched the air with enthusiasm.

Almost six-thirty. Lawrence would have been waiting thirty minutes now at the small square that had been turned into an ice skating rink for the Christmas holidays. There by the markets in front of the big blow-up Santa and fake-snow-covered trees. She couldn't face the Christmas lights wrapped around the trunks of the palm trees, the Santas hanging from the black wrought-iron balconies, the Christmas carols in English from speakers on the streets. Lawrence would have scrolled through his newsfeeds and would now be wondering where she was.

When she and Simon had lived here for six months, Simon had loved preparing the Christmas meal for her while she sat on a bentwood chair (they'd picked up a couple at the Brocante market in Nice) sipping a pastis (no ice for her) and listening to ABC FM through his laptop. They'd both loved hearing the familiar announcers' voices from Australia.

She should get a move on. If she couldn't face trying to converse in French at the market, she should at least cycle over to Super U. She shouldn't keep Lawrence waiting there in the freezing cold. Maybe a cycle after work was being too selfish, but she could feel the endorphins kick in that kept her mood disorder at bay.

When at last she rode to the square in Beaulieu sur Mer, Lawrence was very relieved to see her.

After a big hug and a kiss, she invented a punctured tyre, promised him extra computer time and a friend for a sleepover at the weekend.

She'd tried hard to help him integrate in France. He'd made new friends at the International School and she'd paid for extra squash coaching. The coach said he was a natural. When Lawrence went in for his shower, she'd sat staring at the opening frames of Winston Churchill at eighty, as depicted in *The Crown* as a young Queen Elizabeth struggled with a resentful husband.

As *la Doctoresse* put her feet up on the footstool and leant back, a worrying thought interrupted her deep sense of calm and control. How will she break the news to Simon? Their son is a squash player, not a rugby boy – although Lawrence's new school friends loved it when he gave away his autographed footballs. She'd have to make a stand with Simon. Or maybe she'd find another way to get the message across. He doesn't even know his own son. How many years has it been now? Just like when the marriage guidance counsellor had said to them, you don't know each other.

*

Still looking for Gypsy.

Because people were smoking outside the café, Crystal and Priscilla sat inside, a front table by the window, watching the Saturday morning shoppers at the food market. They were on their way home to meet up with a real estate agent to get a valuation on the newly renovated room ready for rental under the house. Priscilla was going to stay out of the way upstairs with Simon. They'd play a quiet game, nothing that could cause noise concerns downstairs.

Priscilla snatched the complimentary chocolate from her mother's saucer and popped it in her mouth. Crystal smacked her lightly on the wrist, telling her she had her own hot chocolate to enjoy. Priscilla wiped her mouth with the back of her hand as the coffee machine hissed behind them. The noisy carbon-emitting cars and motorbikes throbbed past the window and Priscilla spotted the girl.

She was standing in front of a bread stall across the road, this new shiny-headed Homeless Girl. Had she found a hairbrush? She was talking to a man with a ponytail who was sliding a loaf of bread into a paper bag.

Then he took a small package from under the counter and handed it over. The Homeless Girl leaned in and kissed him on the lips before putting the parcel in her pocket and zipping it up. That was all Priscilla saw before the Homeless Girl hurried off into the crowd, pulling the golden Labrador behind her. She disappeared down Oxford Street smiling with joy.

*

The rest of the world are busy with their lives. Making plans. Going places. There must be something wrong with him. Different. His life felt meaningless.

As soon as he heard the real estate agent start up her car, Simon had gone to the window to inspect the cloudless day and to think more deeply about what was the matter with him. How come he wasn't like other people? Thinking about these things didn't help.

La Doctoresse had said once, 'You aim for one hundred and ten per cent and you're not prepared to settle for ninety.' She was referring to their marriage. And once, consumed with rage, her fists clenched in anger, 'What do you want? Just tell me what you want me to do. Stop? Move? What? I have no role model to follow. I don't know what to do.'

Simon watched a smooth-faced hoody-wearing boy walk past with his mother and bite into a *pain au chocolat*, his mother engrossed with her mobile. The young man reminded him of his own boy so far away in France.

Julian's sleek motorbike pulled up outside. He climbed off and stood looking up at the house, holding his hands to his forehead to shade his eyes from the glare.

Simon moved away from the window.

Julian pressed the front-door buzzer.

*

Simon's twenty-fifth birthday fell or had fallen in January and found him sleeping on the bottom bunk on the overnight train from Xi'an to Shanghai, China: sleeping despite the clang and crash of the track changes in the winter winds from Mongolia.

A small table between the bunks. On top of the table, a scallop-edged white table cloth, a red flower in a thin-necked vase, a flask of hot water, two bottles of mineral water.

He'd cycled from Guangzhou to Guilin with a Cycle China group. All those rice paddies. Not that he noticed much about the scenery; he was concentrating too hard on making it up the next hill. It was tough. Really tough. The locals thought they were crazy, these tourists who paid money to ride a bike. Why would you do that for a holiday, they wondered?

Above him, on the top bunk, slept the female cyclist from Australia, Doctor Sarah. At that time, she'd just finished an acupuncture course in Beijing: Acupuncture As an Aid To Pain Relief. In Guilin when the group had a break from the cycling and had had some cheap clothes made up, Sarah and Simon had conversed at length. He'd told her about the sudden death of his wife and she'd confided in him her feelings of instability and insecurity in this very foreign country.

When he'd discovered they'd been allocated the same sleeping compartment and she'd be above him on the top bunk, he'd warned, 'Don't come down the ladder in the middle of the night wearing only your nightie.'

She'd laughed and told him to drop the ridiculous money belt that was clipped around his waist. 'It looks so ugly sticking out like that,' she said. 'Take it off. And while you're at it, drop your jeans too.'

After, they'd had a shower and then he'd gone off to purchase another two bottles of mineral water.

*

Simon let his mini pool cue fall to the ground and raced out the door, jumped down the front steps to the street, just in time to get to Julian as he revved up his motorbike. Simon stood in front of the Harley, attempting to eyeball Julian through the slit of his helmet.

'Wow! I've never seen anyone jump over so many steps without it ending in tears.'

'You're not aware of my athletic abilities.'

'Yeh. That's for sure.' Julian turned off the ignition, unclipped his helmet and studied this alpha male standing in his path.

'Why don't you come in and cool off by the pool till Crystal gets back.'

*

Expecting a heated exchange, Julian sat by the edge of the pool, his feet immersed in the water.

Simon, after unpegging a Speedo from the clothesline, had opened up the Cabana and gone in to change.

Julian understood Simon's situation. He knew how it was to re-partner and find yourself absent from your own children's lives. He knew what it was like to travel the world in search of a different future. He also knew that you could do that when you're young but one day you had to return home and settle down. That's what he'd done. Where once he was restless, resentful, anguished, now he had For Women With Curves to focus on, and Dina, of course.

Julian glanced up at the kookaburra looking down from its eyrie on the clothesline.

The sun had moved behind a cloud. The water lost its sparkle, a deep container of blue surrounded by trees. Julian watched a spider splayed in its web between the branches of a frangipani tree as the sun began to emerge again.

The clouds drifted off to the east.

The kookaburra looked around one last time and flew away.

Where was Simon? Why was he taking so long? Julian checked the time on his phone. A couple more minutes and then he'd take off.

*

The major challenge for Julian just now had to be how to convince 'Mr Bludging Off a Generous Partner' that taking on a business is just what he needed to do with his life right now.

'It's not something I was planning to do.'

'It would be great to own your own hair salon. You won't have some-one else telling you what's what. You can have holidays whenever you like. You'd be your own boss.'

'As I said, it's not something I'd seen myself doing. But…if you were to come in as a silent partner, maybe it's a possibility.'

'How timel,y the poor salon owner being so ill and making you an offer too good to refuse.'

A surprising turn of events. And didn't Simon realise those yellow Speedos became transparent when wet? Why hadn't Crystal pointed it out to him?

'And why do you think I'd want to be a silent partner?'

Simon wrapped a beach towel around his legs. 'Because you're doing so well with the For Women With Curves thing.'

'That's true,' said Julian.

It wasn't really true, not for now, but he absolutely expected it to be, in the fullness of time.

*

'Wow! That's a turnaround. How did you talk him into it?'

Julian had given Dina a ball by ball description of what had transpired. How Simon was made a fabulous offer from the owner of the salon where he worked who wanted to retire due to health issues. Simon didn't realise he'd definitely make more money if he took over the business.

'I told him I'd help him get an online presence. They sell a lot of hair products in that salon. He suggested I come on board as a silent partner. Lunatic Fringe, he wanted to call it.

Dina thought the name was a great idea but didn't want Julian in-vesting in the salon. If Simon wanted to make some decent money, he needed to do it on his own. And, anyway, Crystal was a smart cookie. She could keep an eye on things.

Dina sucked in a deep breath. What was Julian doing at Crystal's place anyway? She knew all about their high school romance. Dina didn't like him hanging around at Crystal's and getting friendly with that Simon fellow. And she didn't like him going places without telling her. Here she was, stuck with all these deliveries to unpack.

'You love getting in among all that lacy lingerie, darling. You know you're in your element imagining all those more-than-a-handful women trying on our gear.'

'That's what *you* do, not *me*.' Dina kicked a box into the wall and walked out the door.

The phone rang. Julian answered it. He wasn't going to stuff things up with Dina. He knew what side his bread was buttered on. The business and Dina gave meaning and purpose to his life. Work and love. Isn't that what Freud said? The ingredients for a happy and fulfilled existence.

And if he ever had doubts about how things would work out in the future, he was clever enough to keep his mouth shut. Mostly. From time to time, he'd forget to zip up those lips of his and he'd end up in big trouble.

*

Aged twenty-five, Simon woke up on that overnight train to Beijing and, hearing no sound from the other bunks, decided to stay in bed a while to think about his prospects. How lucky he was that Doctor Sarah had chosen him out of all the other guys on the Cycle China trip: the bicycle couriers from Sydney, the triathletes from London, the super-fit Germans. But before he spent any more time thanking his lucky stars, he had to get himself to the men's bathroom.

When he looked down the corridor – the silent sombre corridor – it was to find an unexpected picture of radiance in the person of a woman of a certain age: her hair a glamorous ash blonde, her nails long and squared, her dress a citrus lemon linen, leaning against the wall opposite the ladies' toilet, a frown of impatience on her fine-boned face. Rings glittered on the hand that fingered a necklace of seed pearls, as if praying on a string of rosary beads. A man burst red-faced out of the women's bathroom and hurried down the passageway.

'I nearly bumped into him,' said a young voice, and out came a girl wearing very tight active wear leotards (a second skin, thought Simon) which outlined a pear-shaped bottom divided in half by a G-string.

'Oh darling,' cried the woman, who was, who must be, her mother.

'I was too embarrassed to say anything when he blundered in,' said the girl, who was, Simon saw, a rather plumper version of her mother. 'I didn't know.' She opened her hands, palms upward in a questioning gesture. 'Maybe it was a lady?'

'You must have got a shock, poor darling!' exclaimed the older woman. 'I walked into the men's bathroom once by mistake. With my trainer. Whoops.' Her eyes opened wide to show surprise.

Simon could only hear the odd word as they walked away together with joyous and conspiratorial laughter.

Simon felt a pang of wistfulness for such closeness, then reminded himself that Doctor Sarah was waiting for him in the compartment. He'd buy her one of those seed pearl necklaces when they reached Beijing, or some amethyst stones from the markets, and have something made up.

Tears of gratitude welled in his eyes; made a river down his cheeks. He brushed the water from his face. The drought had ended. He'd been chosen, and by someone intelligent, attractive and successful.

How good could life get, this getting just what you wanted? How blue is the sky? How brightly the stars shine in the night out here.

*

Still looking for Gypsy.

As her know-it-all foster mother had suggested, the Homeless Girl had put a cold washer on her face and positioned herself in front of a fan. Useless bloody fans – all they did was blow the hot air around.

The Homeless Girl listened to the news report warning of catastrophic fire conditions. She took a last drag on her cigarette and flicked the butt out the window.

She'd heard it all before: a careless act by one person, a dropped cigarette, ignitions when the wind speed increased caused by the draught of a line of passing traffic. Well, she wasn't in a car throwing a butt out by the side of the road, was she?

She reached over to the fan on the table under the window and adjusted it to rotate.

Now a southerly had kicked in, she might take Gypsy to the park for a play with the ball.

*

Still looking for Gypsy.

Simon ambled up through Cooper Park gully thinking of other summers. Summers when it rained for days on end and his feet were waterlogged in wet socks and soggy sneakers – this land of droughts and flooding rains. Was that Rosemary hurrying up the stairs, her head and neck leading the way at an angle from her hunched shoulders, willing herself onwards?

He positioned two fingers in his mouth and blew a piercing whistle.

Rosemary turned her suffering face and looked behind her.

'Wait for me,' he shouted.

*

Still looking for Gypsy.

Dina, knotted with anxiety, exhausted from lack of sleep and all the worrying, sat sipping a decaf on the balcony of the café that overlooked the tennis courts at the park. The courts and café were under new management, with a ramp for wheelchair access built to please the council. The cane chairs were very inviting, though Julian reckoned tennis had had its day and the place wouldn't be turning over much money.

For goodness sake! There was Simon with that older woman with the hennaed hair. She'd known he was up to something. What could you expect with one in three marriages ending in divorce? Same story in the bush at Mudgee. And even if people stayed together for the sake of the kids. Her dad, a self-made businessman, wouldn't have given these young people the time of day and nor would her mum, who was well known for the knitted bedsocks she gave away as presents for birthdays and at Christmas. Dina missed her dad, but that was something Julian didn't want to hear.

An attractive young woman walked by with a dog of a kind Dina had often seen on TV being trained to lead a blind person. Dina fell in love with this Labrador instantly. How she longed for them to stop so she could pat him.

Gypsy gazed at Dina and Dina gazed right back as the Homeless Girl plodded heavily by on feet enclosed in sensible sandals with Velcro straps, like something her mum would have worn. A straight black fringe covered her eyebrows and her rosy face had lips painted in the shape of a heart that could only be described as generous and red as the big hoop earrings that dangled from her earlobes.

For some reason, a tear made its way down Dina's cheek and dripped onto her hand.

Dina wondered if she should try and buy her way out of the Women With Curves business with Julian and head back home to Mudgee, a place where she'd wake up to see kangaroos outside her window. Not that she had any way of earning a living in the bush. She thought of her dad, who used to say, 'The funny thing is, life can only be understood backwards yet has to be lived forwards.'

*

At five o'clock, Crystal and Priscilla got off the train a stop early so they could go to the pizza place.

Priscilla chose a table at the front and opened up the menu. Hawaiian for her, vegetarian for Crystal, and a meat lover's to take home for Simon.

Crystal took a block of dark chocolate with added coconut out of her handbag and broke off a square. She offered the block to Priscilla, who pulled a face and said she only ate white chocolate.

Crystal thought the interview with the prospective tenant for the room under the house had gone well. The woman had agreed to pay the rent in cash to avoid Crystal having to pay more money to the tax department.

As she folded the foil over the chocolate bar and returned it to her bag, the idea entered her head that, with some extra cash coming in, she could give Simon more of the undivided attention he craved.

She unwrapped the foil again and broke off another square.

'It will make you fat,' scolded Priscilla from the chair opposite.

Crystal told herself she probably lived in a fantasy world, but what would life be if you didn't have dreams?

She told Priscilla not to speak in that loud rude voice. What would people think?

She'd heard Julian and Dina, fed up with nowhere to park, traffic jams, and city high-rises, were talking of moving to the Blue Mountains, where there was a slower pace of life.

Crystal felt unadventurous and predictable.

Priscilla ate the marshmallow from the saucer beside her hot chocolate and complained in disappointment about being given only one marshmallow, instead of the usual two.

Crystal knew how it felt when your expectations weren't met. Often, she longed for things that were never going to happen, like being able to manifest a sea change. But, put simply, what was the point? To exchange one set of problems for a whole other set? And, besides, you always took yourself with you, wherever you went.

*

'I'm feeling a bit wobbly,' said a young Amelie (the Homeless Girl) in a deadened tone of voice.

Psychiatrist Jane had been able to give unconditional support, to listen with an open mind, and to do her best to raise Amelie's low self-esteem. Psychiatrist Jane had been confident she could help the young Amelie. She'd helped many children to navigate the difficult adolescent years. She was a great believer in mindfulness as a daily practice.

Every Thursday, Amelie would come here, to a house on Oxford Street, so she could tell Psychiatrist Jane about the people and events in her life that had triggered a freefall spiral. They'd have a conversation back and forth until Amelie would lean back in the chair, unburdened. Then the doctor would write the name of a funny television show – for the purpose of relaxation – or the name of a book about how someone manages their mental health, or the latest book on cognitive behavioural therapy on a piece of paper and hand it over. It seemed to help.

*

Early morning sun and illumination from the cane light fitting lit up the café. White coffee cups clinked against matching saucers. On their way to work, customers lined up to place their orders. Madam Betty, the masseur from Beverly Springs Wellness Centre, mounted the stairs, her eyes sweeping the tables for the best place to sit.

Kingston worked the coffee machine, bang bang, compressing coffee grains, frothing milk. Soon all orders would be complete, the water jugs filled, the tables wiped down. Then, Kingston would have the satisfaction of knowing he'd played his part in keeping the customers happy. Betty had told him the hardest part of running a café was getting good staff. It was the same story at the Wellness Centre, she'd said.

Although he refused to stop and give it his full attention, Kingston was aware of a scene going on outside between a man with a dog and a woman. The dog had jumped up on the woman. 'Get that bloody dog away from me,' she'd screamed. The man reminded Kingston of that scrawny piece of work his wife was shacked up with.

Kingston watched as Madam Betty sauntered over to pour herself a glass of water, her handbag disturbing the patrons as she brushed past the tightly packed tables of people whose downcast eyes were absorbed in their mobile phones. She had no eyes for Kingston, it seemed, despite her interest in Netflix and the events of the afternoon when she'd given him special extras as part of the massage and made him so very happy. She'd felt sorry for him, that's all, looking to hone her skills and maybe earn some extra cash.

The scrawny piece of work tied the dog up outside, then sat down at a table as Madam Betty swept past.

She returned to the comfortable couch that ran against the wall.

Kingston, from his position behind the glass cake display, stood at the coffee machine with his back to the customers. How had he managed to get himself a job as a barista? And then he remembered, and breathed out with a loud sigh. And thought with shame of his destructive action with the brick towards his ex-wife, who had shown nothing but patience towards him, and who didn't deserve to be treated like that. I have been motivated by selfishness, he thought, because I don't like another man living in my house. Thanks to my new life here at Beverly Springs Wellness Centre, I now recognise my intolerance, my impatience, my need for validation by others. My need to show Mother (if she were still alive) that she could be proud of me. I am lacking in confidence because of my troubled relationship with Mother and her cruelty, and I am constantly on watch for more. But most women are not like her, and it is really foolish of me to have put Crystal in the same box as Mother.

Kingston, Father would have said, there are three important things in life: good health, a good home, and good parents.

Neither Mother nor Father had comprehended his need to search for a spiritual path. Father thought all religious practices were a load of codswallop and he never stopped saying so. He never understood.

Kingston closed his eyes as those familiar voices from a faint and far off place continued in his head.

'Find a girl with her head screwed on the right way.'

'I found a nice girl, Dad. We set up house together. But it didn't work out.'

'It all fell apart because you dumped your wife and children and headed off to Bali.'

'That's true,' exhaled Kingston, aware that he'd developed a facial tic. 'I couldn't hang in there.'

'Who's to blame, then, if it wasn't you?'

'Why is there always finger pointing? Why can't things just not work out, sometimes? It's no one's fault?'

Kingston opened his eyes. He must have been in a trance.

But then, he bent his head again, overcome by a sense of futility.

*

Still looking for Gypsy.

The moonrise had been brief, caught sight of between the front seats as they'd lain together across the back of the car, Rosemary's feet up on the windows. They were parked there out on the headland at Ben Buckler.

'Not the most comfortable,' Rosemary had said. 'We could splash out next time and get a room.'

Simon rolled off, unable to wipe the grin off his face. He caressed her hair. She held his hand and put it on her heart.

'Well?' he'd asked.

Rosemary hadn't responded. She'd had no desire to tell him about Grace's accident. She felt adrift, disconnected, not able to be present in the moment.

'I'd better get a move on,' she said.

*

Crystal had already eaten the leftover pizza straight from the box after putting Priscilla to bed. She opened up Simon's meat lover's and ate a slice. What she wouldn't have minded just now was a gin and tonic, but who could be bothered? She liked sitting here in the dark at the bay window with the doors and windows closed, cocooned against whatever traffic noise was out there at this time of night, dulled by the double-glazed glass. The television screen flickered next door and their bathroom light lit up the darkness.

She wondered how Kingston was getting on. Hopefully he'd landed on his feet somewhere.

And Simon too. She hoped he was okay, wherever he was.

*

No text from Dina. Nothing.

Why couldn't Julian have kept his opinion to himself and why hadn't he been able convince Dina that it was normal? Like that first Easter when everyone Julian knew was unavailable to go to the music festival in Canberra and Dina had turned up at the front door of his apartment at Tamarama with two festival wristbands and a two-man tent.

Dina had borrowed a couple of sleeping bags, a billycan with clamp, and bought two quick-dry towels from Kathmandu. She'd also bought a new hot-water bottle as an Easter gift for Julian. He had given Dina a stylish Italian-design bread maker.

They'd stood together in the kitchen to have a go at making a batch of rye bread with caraway seeds. It was when he'd untied the apron from around her waist that, for the first time, he'd let his hands explore further.

Then they'd set up the tent on the floor in the lounge room and made love. Afterwards, Dina had giggled because she'd never been intimate with another person in that particular way. She'd found it visually unattractive (all that hair), but had found it to be mutually gratifying.

Julian had been so bowled over by all this unexpected naivety and excitement that had come upon him unexpectedly that he'd failed to hear the warning beeps on the bread maker that were trying to alert them to some burning taking place. But by the time the smoke detector started up and the woman downstairs had begun banging on the ceiling with a broom handle, the romantic ambience had been ruined.

After such a dramatic start to their relationship, Julian felt he had to ask himself why was it that now the fire between them seemed to have gone out.

*

A key turned in the front door lock, making Crystal's heart skip a beat until in walked a man who turned out to be her father, wanting to know if he could bed down for the night in the room under the house. He had travelled down from the Central Coast and was on his way to a holiday on the Colo River, though why he hadn't rung beforehand to say so he didn't disclose.

Crystal had told him he was always welcome to come and stay for a sleepover.

He left his new lightweight travel bag by the door and hurried through the lounge room and into the kitchen to toast a couple of slices of raisin bread.

For five years, he'd rented a caravan for a month on the Colo River, a famous river, the home of bass and platypus, whose name is derived from the Aboriginal word for koala. He always booked the same caravan, which was well located overlooking the wild river.

Crystal wondered about the place. She imagined herself canoeing, bushwalking and swimming, and, in doing so, realised just how wrung-out she felt. She watched her father eat his thickly buttered toast (he'd offered to make her some too but she'd declined) and decided that maybe there were worse things in life than eating carbs after five p.m.

In the caravan park with its view over the water, her father would eat bread and cheese and drink beer and only leave the area to go bush-walking in the Wollemi National Park.

Excitedly, Crystal remembered a bottle of Pinot Noir that stood on the kitchen bench next to the microwave.

'You'll have a ball, Dad,' she said, walking over to pour them both a glass.

Her father stopped his munching. 'So, tell me, where's that man of yours?'

'He's not really *my* man,' said Crystal, pouring herself a second glass. She put the bottle down with a clunk and turned to face her father sitting in her kitchen. She was happy he was there so she could tell someone who was important to her the good news.

'I've got a tenant for downstairs. She moves in next week.' Which wasn't totally true. The woman hadn't signed the contract and handed over the bond yet. 'But don't worry, there'll always be a place for you on the couch.'

He finished eating, stood up, went around the table and put his arm around his daughter. 'See,' he said. 'Good things come to those who wait.' He raised his glass for a toast. 'To my clever daughter.'

'I don't know about that,' mumbled Crystal humbly.

'What? What don't you know?' asked Simon as he ambled in. His shirt hung out loose over his jeans and he wasn't too pleased at seeing a suitcase at the front door and Crystal's dad in the kitchen.

'She's cutting back her workload,' said Crystal's father, 'because she's got a tenant for downstairs and I'm heading off on holidays early in the morning.'

'Where are you going?' asked Simon, walking over to the kettle and filling it with water. He flicked the switch, loosened his belt and tucked his shirt in to his trousers.

'Back to the Colo River,' said Crystal's father, not that Simon was listening.

*

Dina returned home and Julian poured her a Scotch on the rocks that he said worked as well as a Valium. They took their drinks into the bedroom, where they talked for a bit, and then had sex, and after that Dina felt more uncertain about things.

While Dina was still asleep, Julian quietly rolled out of bed before the dawn light made its appearance between the curtains and turned on his computer. He needed to be careful about what he said to Crystal before he fired off an email. With Crystal, you had to be straightforward. What you saw is what you got with her. Crystal had both feet planted firmly on the ground.

'Look, Julian, what happened between you and me was years ago – past history,' was all Crystal had ever had to say about it, sometimes adding, 'We've both moved on with our lives.'

He knew exactly why he'd remained infatuated with Crystal. He regretted that this was so. It's not as if he'd liked being the dominant one – every time. She'd done her best to teach him the benefits of submission.

Julian shut down the computer and took himself into the kitchen to make a double-shot cappuccino. He couldn't be talked into switching over to one of those herbal teas, even though his doctor had said he needed to calm down his nervous system by drinking less caffeine. He wasn't prepared to give up on coffee no matter what anyone said. Where was the shaved chocolate to sprinkle on top? Where had that chocoholic Dina put it, or had she binged on the whole tin again?

*

Simon rode the escalator up to the top floor and walked towards the Café Gallery. The Cycle China group had checked in to a hotel in Beijing before heading out separately to buy take-home presents for loved ones. He went into the coffee shop, took a seat on the back couch and ordered scrambled eggs and coffee. Two dark-suited men talked business in front of him. Simon switched on the data on his mobile and checked Facebook before eating his scrambled eggs. He decided to shop at the department store on the ground floor for a piece of jewellery for Doctor Sarah. On his way out, Simon stopped when he saw a collection of seed pearl necklaces on display. Just what he was looking for. To this day, she still loves that necklace.

*

The morning sun had not yet lightened the night sky. Julian kept glancing out the window as he clicked on Crystal's name in his address book. He sat there a moment, wondering what he'd write, then started typing. Type type click click and Julian was up there with the birds looking down on the outgoing mail server flying very rapidly via the simple mail transfer protocol (SMTP), replicating the local post office, checking the postage and address and working out where Crystal's WiFi lived.

She shot back a reply from her iPhone. 'Piss off, Julian.'

Julian finished his double-shot coffee and found renewed hope in the remnants of milk froth that he scraped up and into his mouth with a spoon. Julian felt out of kilter. Felt his life story change its narrative, a rewrite, become a different drama from a different perspective. It seemed unnatural to have your version of the past discounted by someone you'd been in love with. Crystal rose before him in the light of dawn, remembered forever in her short blue and white chequered school dress and slip-on black platform school shoes.

'Crystal,' he said to the vision, wondering if he had time-travelled to the past and how he'd conduct his life there if this was so. But no problem. It was Dina standing by the window, a golden halo around her in the soft light from the morning sky.

Dina eyeballed him, glancing from the computer screen in front of him to his surprised face. 'So, what's going on?'

How could he tell her that he'd just asked Crystal to meet him for a drink? The differences between the two women – the strong Amazon-woman-Crystal who pulled herself back up after her firstborn ran away and her grieving spiritual-seeker husband leaving her and little Priscilla to go live in Bali, and little Dina Doolittle from Mudgee looking fragile in her baby-pink gingham nightie was more than Julian could bear.

He jumped up from the desk, marched across the hemp rug that stood between them his fists clenched with anger. He gave Dina a shove. 'Fuck you, Dina,' he shouted as she retreated to the bedroom too stunned to think of an appropriate response.

Her body shook with the shock of it. No one had ever spoken to her like that in her life before, and she'd never seen this angry side of Julian. How dare he raise a hand to her. He'd behaved appallingly, and all because she'd asked him a simple question. His unforgiveable response must relate to something else, perhaps the stress of the Women With Curves franchise. It couldn't possibly be because of her. But she could see a turning point in a relationship when it presented itself. The thing was to find somewhere safe to stay for the rest of the night and then reassess the situation in the full light of day.

In the bedroom, she sent a text to her good friend, took off her nightie, pulled on some loose trousers, singlet top and a jacket. She stormed out the back door and crossed the road. Freda let her in and gave her a pillow and some bedding for the couch. Dina knew she should let Julian know where she was, but decided to wait. She understood that Freda was anxious to get back into bed with her husband. She appreciated a place to bunk down until the beginning of the new work day. Freda had offered neighbourly friendship all those months ago when Dina had first moved in with Julian.

In the morning, she told Freda the whole story of what had happened the night before. Freda said it wasn't so bad; she and her husband often shouted 'Fuck you' at each other. She said Dina was lucky if she hadn't been spoken to like that before. And what was a little shove? It wasn't as if he hit her. Toughen up, girl. Dina tried to explain that the use of her name after the 'Fuck you' had been especially hurtful.

*

Crystal's dad was throwing a line into the Colo River with his special lady friend who rented a caravan at the same time each year in the same place as he did, when his daughter called to tell him that Julian had agreed to mentor Simon to help get a business plan together for the Lunatic Fringe salon idea.

Dave was pleased to hear that that bludger Simon was going to get off his butt and take on some responsibility for a change. About time. Dave remembered Julian from Crystal's high school days. He'd seemed a decent chap. Dave was so happy to hear the news he suggested to his special lady friend that they go back to his caravan for a couple of celebratory beers (or maybe a just-for-special-occasions joint).

'Sure,' she said. 'No point in getting pissed all on your own.'

*

An impending downer pulls *la Doctoresse de Anti-ageing*'s rollercoaster emotional life out of the apartment with raincoat and umbrella and on her way to meet with *le Professeur* for a meaningful conversation. The clouds do their best to drench her as she makes the ascent to the Moyenne Corniche before the final climb up to Mont Boron, where they will rendezvous in the car park above Nice. She wants to tell him face to face that she won't be coming to his house to play table tennis while his wife is away. She knows he'll say she's old-fashioned, but she doesn't care. He's a married man.

*

Still looking for Gypsy.

Rosemary doesn't know how to talk to Philip any more. What had happened to them? Why this constant bickering and point scoring? All she could think about was being with Simon at Ben Buckler. She must see him as a matter of the greatest urgency. Today? Tonight? What exactly does she want from him?

82

Today she'll be at the hospital watching over Grace.

'Something's going on,' said Philip to himself when Rosemary had put on her coat and left the house. 'Some other bloke who's prepared to talk with her about the meaning of life till the cows come home,' and he opened his book after pouring himself another cup of tea from their sterling silver teapot, grown old and discoloured from lack of loving care.

*

Kingston leans against the coffee machine watching the busy shoppers hurry to their destinations and, finding little distraction there, he scrolls through his Snapchat feed.

A distant busker's violin, heavy breathing – is it the boss at the cash register behind him? Or it may be the release of his own breath that he hears.

Seated on the walkway outside the café at an industrial-look metal chair and table, comes the loud voice of the man with the dog talking on his mobile to his stockbroker about the movement of shares.

'Twenty-nine and a half? Worth the wait? Big parcels. Huge quantities. I'll leave it with you.'

Shares. That's the way to go, thinks Kingston as he unstacks the dishwasher, wipes the glassware. If only he'd invested in bank shares with the insurance money rather than all that travelling.

The dog has stretched himself out with his chin on the ground but looks over his nose, his floppy ears moving up and around like antennae. His master walks into the café.

'Soy cap, isn't it?' asks Kingston.

'Yes. Great. Thanks.'

An older woman walks in.

'How's it going, Bonnie? Looks like the rain is easing.'

'Better rain than that heat,' she says. 'Although it's the humidity that gets to me, rather than the heat.'

'You want a coffee? With toast?'

She shakes her head. 'No. No. Just a coffee.'

Across from the café, people head into the post office to join the long queue – and it's not even Christmas.

Betty the masseuse walks in.

'Hello, gorgeous,' says Kingston.

'Flattery will get you everywhere,' she croons.

Betty turns to the woman behind her to support this statement, but the woman, unwilling to get involved in public discourse, has jumped the queue and stands in front of the boss at the cash register ready to place her order. On the counter beside the boss is a poem written in chalk on a small blackboard.

> I like my coffee
> How I like myself
> Dark, bitter, and
> Too hot for you!

When Madam Betty departs, Kingston calls out to her, 'Goodby,e darling. Have a great day. May the force be with you.'

She smiles back at him.

'Be careful, Kingston,' warns the boss. 'Don't stuff up. This job could be your path to redemption.'

*

Dina looked up at the ferns in baskets hanging from the ceiling above the couch and decided that as soon as the sun rose above the escarpment she'd make her way back across the road. Julian would be wondering where she'd got to, and there'd be heaps of work to be done for end of financial year for Women With Curves. It was expected the business would make a decent profit, once those invoices were sent out.

Dina left Freda's house that morning to return to her old life while Freda was still asleep. Better the devil you know than the devil you don't know, was Freda's advice.

Dina pulled a new tub of sweet-smelling hand cream out of her bag and left it on the table as a parting gift for Freda, who had been so welcoming in this time of need.

When Dina had left, Freda removed the lid of the cream and inhaled geranium and patchouli. She liked its rich creamy texture. 'Good luck, Dina,' she said out loud. 'You'll need more than a nice hand cream to smooth your way through life with that Julian.

'Well, you're doing all right, love,' said Freda's husband from the kitchen. 'You know how to keep a man happy.'

Freda raised two fingers to her head and pretended to shoot herself.

*

Still looking for Gypsy.

And, 'Shit' says the Homeless Girl.

She has cut herself opening a large can of beetroot. Serves her right for choosing something so healthy. She rummages through the kitchen drawer and searches unsuccessfully through the cutlery for a bandage. That's where her foster mother keeps the matches, why not the bandages?

She goes out the back to the shed to see if her foster father can shine some light on the situation. She knows he is in there because that's where he always is.

He opens up.

His name is Christian.

A kind man, thinks the Homeless Girl. That's what this warmth in the chest must be.

'Come on in,' says Christian, hoping she has come to learn some useful carpentry skills. He shuts the door.

Gypsy, who has followed his mistress out to the back of the house, extends his two front paws in through the gap beneath the door and whines.

*

This being the fourth Tuesday of the month, Kelly, with bucket and mop, had let herself in through the back. She hadn't yet popped her head around the door of Philip's study because she'd run out of suitable greetings to offer a man whose only daughter still lay in a hospital bed, and anyway, Philip's need for a long chat makes her run late for her next job.

Philip heard the sharp slap of the metal bucket hit the tiles which meant Kelly was about to mop the back steps. The steps Grace used to run up when she would come home from school; the corridor crowded with bicycles, skateboards and Grace's surfboard. The steep back steps with the cobwebs where, on expansive February evenings, it is not unusual for Philip to stand at one or other of the railings or landings to watch the fragile white moons of summer hang high in the sky, so high as to be in danger of colliding with the stars overhead and then a tide of white suffering would shatter the lethal spiderwebs in Cooper Park and engulf them all beneath warm skies spread with those laughing kookaburras.

*

Crystal trudged down the stairs to the rubbish bins by the side of the house, the empty stinking tuna tins in knotted plastic bags, and who should she see walking up the front path but Julian with an anguished look on his face because Dina, apparently, had accused him of psychological abuse. Also, Dina was adamant about Julian not investing in Simon's idea to take over ownership of the hair salon.

Julian was keen for Crystal to give him some of her wise-woman counsel.

Crystal let Julian know that investing in Simon's plan was not necessarily a sound financial decision. She told Julian he could come in for a cup of tea and talk things through, although she was anxious to get out of the house and down the road to see if she could get a walk-in appointment for a pedicure. She was desperate for some tender self-care.

'Dina's got her knickers in a knot,' said Julian, his voice rising in pitch as it usually did when he'd lost control of life's unfolding events.

Crystal wondered what she'd ever seen in the man. She thought of Simon out the back mowing the lawn sweating like a pig in his Aged to Perfection T-shirt, his misshapen knobbly toes sticking out of those hippy sandals, and it occurred to Crystal that she'd gone off men, for now.

Later in the morning, Julian went back home and Crystal sent Priscila out to rake up the grass while she went to have a word with that secretive Simon.

*

Just before Julian gets back home, the landline rings for Dina. The sound of Freda-from-across-the-road's upbeat warm and friendly voice gives her a much-needed boost.

Freda is cooking up a batch of sourdough Easter buns; would Dina like to come over? And she's been experimenting with a turmeric latte recipe. Would Dina like to give it the taste test? And don't forget the granny flat out the back that is without a tenant just now. Come on over and check the room out.

'I'll be right there,' says Dina.

*

Still looking for Gypsy.

Philip, flat on his back on the bed, listens to a relaxation tape. Kelly doesn't disturb him. She picks up the $100 note from under the fruit bowl on the dining room table and quietly backs out the door with her bucket and mop.

Philip won't visit the hospital this afternoon. When a Tibetan bell sounds the completion of Track 2, he will decide to walk up to Bondi Junction and buy a barbecue chicken for dinner. Then he will make a green salad and set the table.

The twins will be happy to sit around for a family meal, but he won't be surprised if Rosemary doesn't turn up in time for dinner.

*

Crystal enters the steam-filled bathroom where Simon is taking a shower.

Simon freezes in terror. He imagines Hitchcock's famous shower scene in *Psycho*. Someone is out to get him, to make him pay for his past transgressions. Is it *la Doctoresse de Anti-ageing* come to punish him, here now, in all his naked vulnerability? Does she want to exact revenge on him for being a rotten husband and rotten father? For his hedonism? For being the kind of man he is, a man always wanting more. He has to face this reality: there is no one to blame but his own restless self. Will she ever forgive him? Can he forgive himself?

Simon grabs a towel and makes a dash for the door.

Crystal unlatches the windows and pushes them open.

*

Je t'aime sings *le Doctoresse of Anti-ageing*'s pulsating heart as she walks back down the mountain near Nice that overlooks the winter turquoise of the Mediterranean. The spectacular panorama forces her to stop and take a photograph.

Because the Sunday Brocante Market is taking place down at the port, she uses an alleyway to get back to her apartment. But first she'll visit the Tabac to buy a phone card so she can make a long phone call to Australia. She wants a good heart-to-heart conversation with her ex-husband Simon. She has realised she took him for granted and, in fact, misses him terribly.

While she's opening up and telling him the depth of her feelings, young Lawrence will be on the bus with the squash team of the International School of Nice.

*

This is how the movie ends: an epic battle between puppies and babies to prevent the launch of a new product that would severely limit the amount of love in the world for babies. The film had been streamed on Priscilla's iPad.

Energised and ready for battle on the grass, Priscilla-the-warrior stands on guard using a tree branch as a weapon. She's Boss Baby in a war between babies and puppies.

Simon hurtles down the stairs and hurries into the newly renovated room under the house and closes the door.

Priscilla scowls, wondering why a grown-up would be so frightened.

Above her, at the bathroom window, Crystal looks down to see what's going on. She watches as Simon makes a hasty retreat and the door closes.

What's wrong with the man? Is he seeing ghosts from the past? Does he think there's a bogeyman out to get him? She has a warm heart. If there's something on his mind that needs to be talked about, all he has to do is open up and be honest.

'Maybe the man's afraid his ex-wife has returned to make him pay for his transgressions,' says Julian from the bathroom door, where he's arrived unannounced.

Crystal jumps in surprise.

Julian had driven all the way home before realising he didn't have his mobile. 'I came back to look for it,' he says, moving towards Crystal at the window. 'Men! You know what we're like.'

He's so near, he's able to put his arms around her and pull her close. Her body responds in a warm and welcoming manner as she remembers the two of them in the bush down by the creek on those long hot afternoons after school.

Julian assumes he's doing a good deed by cheering her up. He kisses her on the cheek and then lets his lips edge towards her mouth. It's a long kiss.

Sometime later, Crystal and Julian search around the house, but can't find his mobile anywhere. Julian says he'll have a more thorough check in his car. Maybe the phone fell out of his pocket while he was driving.

*

Still looking for Gypsy.

It's deadly quiet in this room. Lifeless. Outside in Cooper Park, people play tennis, their coaches armed with baskets of tennis balls.

A dull light through the dirt-streaked window. Dead and dying flowers in the clear glass vase on the ledge.

A fly crawls up the windowpane then circles around and around Simon's head. Where to from here? he wonders.

A woman with furrowed brow strides up through the park, her ears plugged by headphones. Simon can hear the thwonk of tennis balls being hit and see the players on the courts. He's never looked out at the world from this angle before.

The voices of the women not wanting to be put in a set with weaker players rises in pitch. The tennis coach is trying to sort it out. They are very badly behaved, those women. Don't they realise how lucky they are to have a former tennis champion to support and encourage them? They can organise their own tennis partners and book their own courts if they don't like the way he does things in the weekly tennis round robin.

*

Kingston wants a full-time job. He hopes the café will extend his hours so he can earn a decent wage. And the daily structure that a regular job provides would do him good. He's sick of being a volunteer in the kitchen preparing the vegetables at Beverly Springs Wellness Centre.

On the blackboard behind him:

> Every new morning is a
> blessing and an opportunity

to allow yourself to be filled
with the desire and passion
to pursue your dreams…

Kingston is proud of himself for finding a new path in life. He enjoys chatting with the café customers and improving his speed as a barista. He doesn't have to blame his family any more for his lack of direction in life. Betty the masseuse agrees with him. Clearly, she's got his back. She had been very supportive from the start by encouraging him to move on from his volunteer work and start earning money. She'd continued to help release the old stresses and tensions from his body with regular massage. He was relaxing into the benefits of having his muscles and tendons stretched and the feel of unconditional love emanate from a pair of nurturing hands.

Betty said maybe in the fullness of time they could rent a place together in Katoomba so they could both save money.

*

Still looking for Gypsy.
What is the Homeless Girl doing in the shed out the back?
Why is her foster father yelling at her?
Why is Gypsy barking outside the door?
Why is smoke coming out the window?
And where are the psychiatric workers from outpatients?
Why is so much that happens in life due to luck and timing?
Then comes a very loud noise.

*

It's nearly time for Grace to open her eyes again.
Can she muster the strength to re-engage with the world? She knows that her parents and little brothers have been gathering there most days beside her hospital bed.

She needs to wake up. But it's so nice not to have a care in the world. Just lying here in the morning sunshine, like a cat who has found its perfectly aligned hot spot and is now asleep along a ley line path.

To keep lying here enjoying the warmth or to re-emerge into life?

She likes being just where she is but she'd love to feel her little brothers' arms around her neck again, feel their weight on her hips. Before the accident, she'd been the big-sister-helper, spoon feeding one of the boys in the high chair while balancing the other boy on her hip.

She doesn't have to make any decisions yet. Her brain is resting after making contact with the pavement. When it has rested enough, she'll wake up.

*

Priscilla had borrowed Julian's phone to take a selfie to remind him that she and her mother are a package deal and, when she had, she'd called out to Crystal to come and see what she'd done.

As they walked up to the school together, they could hear the children singing already. Late as usual.

Priscilla linked arms with her mother. 'I dreamed you were a puppet with strings and that a man was making you dance,' Priscilla told her.

Crystal gave her wise daughter a kiss on the head. There were never enough kisses and hugs to give that girl.

At the weekend, they'd get out their wetsuits and go snorkelling at Clovelly. They might even sight the famous groper fish again. Crystal needed to think clearly about things, and immersing herself in the cold ocean was exactly what she needed to do.

*

Simon secures his tracksuit top. It's time to get out of here. He zips the jacket up to his wordless throat as the thick grey cloudless sky hangs low above him.

Men in suits, neatly pressed white shirts and skinny ties, their hair closely cropped at the sides and gelled on top, stand at the bus stop looking down at their phones lest someone make eye contact with them.

As Simon nears, a stretch bus vomits a dark cloud of exhaust so noxious he turns away. Schoolchildren loaded with massive backpacks hurry by. Active-wear glad gym junkies cradle their coffees.

What's the rush?

Police in high-vis jackets, serious faces and breath-test devices signal selected drivers to pull over to the side of the road.

Is life happening without him?

*

The Homeless Girl's foster father hadn't expected to die so young.

For most of his life, he'd felt ten feet tall and invincible. He'd always looked after himself: no smoking, moderate drinking, a yearly visit to the GP.

'Only the good die young,' his mother used to say.

It didn't seem fair. Not now.

*

Still looking for Gypsy.

Fiery autumn leaves crunch underfoot as he hurries down the street. Simon, who is in no frame of mind to appreciate the beauty of nature, ignores the pedestrian crossing and makes a dash for it between the cars to the other side of the road.

On he goes past the cafés and stylish women's clothing stores side by side – window after window. How do all these places pay the rent? Who buys this stuff? 'Shopping gives women a pick-me-up,' says Simon to himself as he enters a room where a thick green border of fake leaves in planter boxes defines the space and emerges out the back to an atrium where Rosemary sits waiting for her coffee at a sunny table in the corner.

'We should get us a room,' Simon says.

Mm. Maybe. Why not? She gives him the nod.

*

I'll show you how the Allen keys work. The Homeless Girl is in the shed with her foster father looking in the storage drawers at the neatly laid out hammers, tape measures, squares, bubble levels, utility knives, marking tools and screwdrivers. Her foster father explains the Allen key wrench is used to drive in bolts and screws, those that have hexagonal sockets in their heads. Well, thinks the Homeless Girl, struggling to remember the name of each tool. Well, well, well. Mr Know-it-all. She closes the drawers back up where he'd left them ajar. Lucky for him she'd been a witness to his true perverse inclinations. If that's the kind of man he is, they're all better off without him.

*

'You're throwing your life away!' Simon had shouted, taking Doctor Sarah by the lapel of her lightweight and easy-to-pack fluffy vest, outside the sourdough bread stand at the fresh food market on Avenue Albert. He pulled her towards him. She'd done something different to her eyebrows, while he'd been busy with other things. Dark. Very dark. Had she tattooed them? And she'd enrolled in yet another course too, at that Anti-ageing Clinic in Monaco. What for, for goodness sake?

'Because we're all doing the best we can with the limited resources and knowledge we have,' Sarah had said.

What kind of answer was that? Did she need even more medical qualifications? They were interviewing this morning, as a matter of fact. Her appointment was at ten-thirty. But she needed to get to the gym first. Get changed, secure her favourite position in the room. Which was why Sarah had to make a move right now.

'Don't you realise you're ruining the lives of three people? Don't you realise that family is everything? You promised forever and ever,' begged Simon.

'Look, Simon. You know as well as I do – we're both miserable. The counsellor said we're destroying each other – one of us will end up in hospital. I thought that person would be me.'

'Here. Take the bloody keys. You have it. Take it all.'

'No need to make a big scene, here in the middle of the road.'

'You've got everything else. You may as well have the apartment too, and all our stuff,' cried Simon.

'Oh, for goodness sake,' sighed Sarah. 'No need for tantrums.'

No one spoke then for some minutes.

Sarah had had this pained expression on her face, like she had just given someone a pap smear. Why did Simon have to make a scene in front of their French neighbours, all here at the village market day? Was it because he had an inflated sense of self-entitlement? What would the professors think of her in Monaco if they knew she had a madman for a husband?

A man with a black briefcase squinted into the sun on the sidewalk, thick wool jacket unzipped. He was talking to a woman with intensity, whose white-blonde hair was secured to the top of her head with a pink flower. Birds sang to each other in the trees above them. The man and woman kissed left right left, and prepared to depart to opposite sides of the road. The couple created just the sort of picture Sarah needed to make her escape.

'We can be loving friends,' she said gently.

'You mean friends with benefits?'

'No. Two people who care about each other very much, who have a long history together.'

'Oh.' Simon let go of Sarah and glanced at the man and woman as they hugged each other before walking off in their separate directions.

Sarah, who still cared deeply for Simon, despite his unreliability and other shortcomings, reached out and plucked a stray hair from his lapel. 'Relationships come to an end, honey. We've grown in different directions, not grown together. It's tough for me too,' she added, which wasn't a lie.

'I don't want to end up old and alone,' cried Simon.

'No chance of that happening,' laughed Sarah. 'Not to a man who loves women the way you do.' Wanting to move forward into a new life, she kissed him goodbye and hurried off.

He watched her walk toward the morning sun until the light became so bright, he had to turn away. What the hell was he meant to do now?

Other people and their lives presented no interest to him as he sat at a sidewalk café biting into an almond croissant. Was it true that love was the food of life? 'Love for sale,' boomed a French voice from the speakers as the café owner's adolescent son balanced a coffee from kitchen to table concentrating hard on not spilling the flat white. Roadwork shattered the silence. The boy placed the cup down with great care in front of Simon. For some reason, the fact the boy managed the task without spilling a drop into the saucer made Simon feel more hopeful.

He began to feel something like pity for Sarah. If what she wanted was to spend the rest of her life working twenty-four-seven with no-one to give her a hand at home, what could he do? She'd chosen her bed… It's not as if he hadn't done his best to help her.

Paris. Paris, the city of love, Simon grumbled to himself. He'd find new inspiration there. His poetry muse often visited him in France; she would come to him again, even without Sarah, although the muse could visit him anywhere.

*

Guilt sits heavily on her chest. It churns away as the days go by. She didn't realise how quiet and empty the apartment would feel without Simon, even with Lawrence still at home and needing to be fed and supervised and driven around. On this particular day, the sounds of the roadworks have increased as more of the bitumen is blasted up and police direct traffic around the obstacles. The sky is a clear blue overhead; dependable in its protective covering of the world.

La Doctoresse of Anti-ageing straddles her bicycle and begins her commute into Monaco. She's not looking forward to the coming summer on the Côte d'Azur. The tourists blocking the streets and filling the shops and restaurants and buses. A stretch bus rumbles past as a workman holds up a Slow sign on the now one-way carriageway. The traffic is slowed and calmed until impatient horns start up their beeping.

Patience, she tells herself. These things take time.

*

'Make a new start somewhere,' Sarah had said.

Well, Simon is doing the best he can under the circumstances. He's standing in a queue at Gare de Nice waiting to purchase a ticket to go up north somewhere: Calais, Paris? And from there he can easily cross the channel to London – if he feels like it. You can't make a start newer than in a city like Paris or London.

*

Sarah, invigorated from her bike ride in the clear Mediterranean air, is telling ten-year-old Lawrence that Dad will spend time with him in the school holidays. Lawrence clutches at his stomach when Sarah tells him that his dad and mum don't love each other any more.

Simon could see Sarah making Lawrence a soothing cup of hot chocolate or some other sugary treat while their dog, one of those fluffy yappy kinds that Simon had taken for a walk twice a day without fail, looked on. Sarah tells Lawrence he'll need to take responsibility now for feeding and walking his dog.

So much for what Simon is able to imagine as he waits in the café at the station. He's seated next to a young couple playing footsies under the table. Their eyes never leave each other's faces. Enraptured.

'Do you mind if I sit here?' he'd asked the young woman, indicating with a nod her bag on the chair beside them. 'It's a bit dark behind the

97

column,' he apologised, indicating the table with no sky visible through the glass.

He sat down beside the couple, and, in an attempt to show them he wasn't listening to the intimacies of their conversation, pulled out his phone and scrolled through social media.

At the ticket counter, he'd made a snap decision and asked for a seat all the way to London. So that's where he ended up, in due course, before he'd flown back home to Australia.

*

Crystal said she'd set up a tent in the lounge room. Priscilla wanted to help. They pulled the tent out of its bag and spread all the parts out on the floor. They could just as well have used the beach shade that could spring up with one flick – a lot easier to set up – but Priscilla had so very much wanted to pretend they were out camping in the bush. Crystal had agreed in the end because she felt bad that a stranger was moving into their room under the house and Priscilla would have to share the front yard and they would lose some of their privacy. Besides, Crystal liked the thought of just the two of them in the tent for the night. She had no idea when Simon would be home. Before the birth of children, she and Kingston would drive away most weekends for a sleepout under the stars. So where was Kingston these days? She really must make some enquiries, in case Priscilla started asking questions about her dad again.

It didn't take them long to get the tent erected and then drag in two mattresses from the playroom. Priscilla had handed the pieces to Crystal as she needed them, following the directions on the diagram. Who knew when Simon would eventually come home? And when he did, he could go upstairs and have the double bed all to himself.

They could have camped out in the backyard, but it was too icy this wintry evening. And severe cold often set off Priscilla's nose bleeds.

Crystal still hadn't had a chance to connect her new printer. Can't be helped. She could work all that out another day.

The second Priscilla crawled into the tent, the dog and cat followed her in. That would make four bodies sleeping in the small space for the night.

'What do you want for dinner, little one?' Crystal asked. 'A cream cheese bagel or those mini meat pies?'

No answer. She opened the flap and there was Priscilla asleep under the cream wool blanket Poppy had given her for her birthday. Crystal would have liked one too but her father had said he only bought presents for children these days, not grown-ups.

Crystal decided there was no point in waiting up for Simon. He seemed distracted by a life elsewhere. She had made a decision to give him as much rope as he needed, which was not like her at all.

The flame from the fake fire flickered along the brick wall. Crystal sat in the tent beside Priscilla, gently pushing the hair back off her face. Priscilla seemed less adventurous these days. Not so long ago, she'd been concerned when Priscilla would take off out the front gate for long stretches of time, taking various multicoloured straws with her. Those expensive bright fluoro straws with the small scoop down one end. Crystal reached out her hand and stroked Priscilla's soft cheek in gratitude and prayer: please stay safe and please don't lose your sense of wonder and curiosity. The cat started up his purring and settled in against the belly of the dog.

She had always been a positive person and firmly believed that Simon would come home to her when he was ready.

Later that evening, Julian sent a text to ask how things were going. She was happy to hear from him. She sent a reply telling him about their plan to sleep in the tent that night. Julian said it sounded like fun and he'd love to sleep under the stars with her one day. Crystal said that wasn't a likely scenario and tried to sound flippant while feeling a stir of excitement at the prospect. It had been good getting together with Julian again after such a long time. All the same, when she'd sent another text, Crystal felt she needed to be careful what she said to him. Exciting is exciting, but she hoped Julian wasn't expecting that it would happen again.

Another incoming text sounded. Oh no, don't tell me he's going to keep at it, but it was from Simon this time, saying don't wait up. He'd be late. But please leave the outside light on.

*

'Mm, impressive,' thought the Homeless Girl and opened up the tray of sparkling spanners again.

'A wrench, or spanner, is a tool used to provide grip and mechanical advantage in applying torque to turn objects – usually rotary fasteners, such as nuts and bolts – or keep them from turning.'

His own special spanner box. Very precious to him, she could tell.

She'd spent the afternoon trying each one out as an instrument of torture. It had seemed difficult at first.

'As the spanner turns, it allows you to apply torque and tighten the nut onto the bolt.'

But things had become more complex as she reached the smaller heads. She wondered why he bothered to have so many. Why didn't he just get a handyman in? One of those older dudes from the Men's Shed.

'Ring spanners grip a fastener at the corners just like a socket spanner,' recited The Homeless Girl. That would do, wouldn't it? Enough punishment for one day for one particular man.

*

A snorting sound on the other side of the bed informed him that she had fallen asleep.

The rhythm of Betty the masseur's breath was interrupted every now and then by twenty seconds of silence, followed by a gasping noise.

Kingston closed his eyes and then opened them again. He tugged at the bed covers, and wished he hadn't offered her a place to sleep for the night when she'd said she didn't want to drive the ten kilometres home to Wentworth Falls through the dark and cold of a thick mountain fog. The thing was, he preferred being alone in his own space. He was used to it now and longed to return to the privacy of his head where he could imagine himself lying on a deserted beach under the shade of a palm tree.

'Hey,' she called out, and yanked at the doona.

Minutes later, the snoring began again. Her tone of voice had upset his reverie. Her words extinguished the vision from his mind. He could only reproduce it if he imagined sawing a hole in the floor of the room, securing a rope ladder to its edges, and climbing down to a sandy beach with one umbrella visible on the sand.

'Give a girl some space,' Betty mumbled and crashed back to sleep.

Kingston thought it was a good thing he was finding out what it would be like to spend long periods of time with another human being before he had any further discussions with Betty about sharing a place together. Could he live with a woman again?

Kingston's father used to tell him stories about how the other inmates told him they had a plan to tunnel out of prison. They were secretly chipping away at their cells.

'You don't want to believe everything people tell you,' he'd advised his father, not wanting his dad to be caught and sentenced to even more time in gaol. But his father was a man not interested in other people's opinions, especially Kingston's. He'd bellow some new humiliation at the boy. It was easy for Kingston to picture his father's face in his head, because he was always there coming in loud and clear: his sniggering and demeaning verbal attacks. The question was, how to get him out of there.

Kingston was starting to realise it was his inner demons that had led him to be a loner. But he liked to tell people that he felt pretty comfortable in his aloneness.

Betty rolled over to his side of the bed, a move that unsettled him. Could she feel him shivering? She put an arm around him. Sure, he'd said she could bunk down for the night because a heavy mist had descended on the mountains. It looked really spooky out there, but that's all he'd agreed to.

'If we snuggled up together, we'd both stay warm.'

Kingston, however, knew about women and their need to control and manipulate. He preferred to keep himself apart. And besides, he didn't want to take any more risks. It's not as if he was looking for anyone.

'Not,' he hissed.

'You're such a funny fellow,' said Betty. 'A crazy-mixed-up-kid. You know that, don't you? I'm sure I'm not the first one to tell you.'

*

Still looking for Gypsy.

Rosemary stood in the kitchenette at the Hilton Hotel watching Simon butter toast. He'd said he couldn't participate in any activities until he had something to eat, which, considering the way his hands shook from a low blood sugar level, seemed a good idea.

She'd had a bit of a time of it getting him in past reception looking so out of it, but Simon had this charismatic demeanour about him that could charm anyone. Now she couldn't help thinking she was being a stupid idiot. She had so much to lose. She'd never participated in anything so foolish in all of the twenty years of her marriage, so why put life as she knew it on the line?

Rosemary untied her scarf and looked deep inside herself for an indication of what was motivating her to risk everything. Disappointment? Had her expectations of Philip been too high? Was that it? Disappointment at him for refusing to let her in to his world since Grace's accident, refusing her the chance to listen to him, and to be listened to. Disappointment doesn't seem a good enough reason to shack-up in a hotel room with someone who is not your husband.

Simon added a smear of Vegemite to his hot buttered toast.

She wished he'd finish with the eating, and finally he did, the side of his mouth stained with Vegemite until he grabbed a serviette and wiped his face. His features revealed themselves to her clean and appealing.

He picked up the room service menu and scanned the list before sinking back on the couch. 'It's a bit overheated in here,' he said and stretched his arms up to pull off his hoody before tossing it on the floor. A lean body exposed itself. Impressive. A six-pack stomach.

Philip wasn't looking too bad for a man his age, though. Why hadn't she reassured Philip recently that women still looked at him with desire in their eyes? He couldn't read a woman's mind, could he?

Once, at Bronte and not long before their wedding day, she had come upon Philip at an open-air restaurant opposite the beach, dramatic as hell in the changing light of dusk, and stopped to get a good look at him before he caught sight of her. To marvel at him, for it had been astonishing to her to see him there in his peaked cap chatting to a man with a dog at the wooden table. His voice had floated to her on the pink blush of the sunset.

The voluptuous clouds had shape-shifted above them as Philip, outlined by the gold of the setting sun, had leapt up from the table, enfolded her in his arms and pushed his mouth against her willing lips.

She wondered if Grace had been with a boy yet, or maybe a girl? Perhaps. Maybe that girl she was with when the accident happened. Was she more than a friend? – although she thought it was probably just the usual intensity of having a teenage best friend.

Rosemary hung her jacket on the back of a chair and removed her scarf.

'Sit down,' said Simon. 'Relax.'

'That's what I'm doing,' she said, easing down beside him on to the couch.

'Plenty of time,' said Simon.

'Yes, the night is still young.'

*

What was she meant to do now? Nervousness made her giggle like a schoolgirl. Should she take a layer of clothing off too and toss it on the floor? Was that being presumptuous? It had been such a long time since she'd flirted with a man, she'd forgotten the moves. Who does what to whom, when? Rosemary wondered if she wasn't too old for this silliness. She didn't even own lace underwear and no one except Philip had seen her naked since before the birth of their children. She automatically pulled her stomach in when she thought of how her body must look to him. She was, she thought, no longer a spring chicken.

She drew in a deep breath, looked across at Simon, her index finger pushing back the cuticle of her thumb. 'My mother always said that youth is wasted on the young.'

'My mother used to say the same thing,' laughed Simon.

Feeling a little better, Rosemary laid her head on his shoulder. He leaned down over her and kissed her hair, wrapping his arms around her like that night when she'd found herself lying on the back seat of his car with her feet up on the windows at Ben Buckler. He reached for the remote, clicked the television off, extended a hand to help her up, guided her down the now dark hallway and finally, confidently, into the bedroom.

*

The twins banged their spoons on the dinner table from their high chairs, doing their best to get Philip to hurry up with the chicken soup. Philip, however, needed to de-stress with a calming shot or two of Scotch.

'Dadda,' wailed the older-by-one-minute Sebastian.

'Don't drink too much,' Philip told himself. 'These boys still need to be bathed and changed and put to bed.'

'Mumma,' wailed Ethan.

Sebastian made a grab for his brother's bare toes, attempting to pull Ethan's foot into his mouth. Ethan used the opportunity to pull the dummy out of Sebastian's mouth and put it in his own.

'Oh, for goodness sake,' said Philip as Sebastian leant over and grabbed the dummy back.

Quick as a flash, Ethan snatched it again. Sebastian cried out, looking to his father for rescue.

Where did Ethan get that determination? wondered Philip. Sebastian, such a gentle sensitive soul. Ethan, so stubborn – just like his mother. He assumed sharing their germs on the dummy was okay, although Rosemary might have a different opinion. At least she wasn't there nagging him about the whisky. Why shouldn't he enjoy the occasional drink?

Was the truth of the situation, in fact, that he, Philip was also sharing? Sharing his wife with another man?

Sebastian opened his mouth and roared, his face scarlet.

'It's okay, boys, dinner is nearly ready.' So much harder without big sister Grace to give a hand with the children while Rosemary was out living it up. His darling Grace would be back with them again before too long.

Philip felt his own anger rise through his body, although rage was more the word for it. It built up inside him. Philip and the chicken soup had been simmering. He'd had a lid on both, although the rage threatened to bubble over.

'I'll give you ice cream for dessert if you eat all your dinner,' he bargained with his sons as he placed a bowl of lukewarm thick chicken and vegetables in front of each boy.

The twins struggled to manoeuvre food into their mouths with spoons. Far easier to pick out chunks of carrot and chicken with their fingers.

'What's the word for it?' Philip muttered through clenched teeth, desperate to swallow a primal scream escaping through his lips. 'Cuckold,' he howled.

The sudden loud sound made Sebastian cry again, which set Ethan off.

Why shouldn't we all have a cry? Grace refusing to speak to him in her hospital bed, Rosemary out testing the boundaries of their marriage.

'Mum, Mum,' yelled Ethan.

Sebastian, who loved his father very much, let out another wail. 'Dadda.'

One parent, two toddlers. The ratio was out of whack. No wonder he needed another Scotch. Oh hell, thought Philip, is it all my fault? Was Rosemary a deluded fool? That man she meets up with has a partner – and a child. Philip got up and returned to the stove, to soak the soup saucepan in hot water that more fortunate men than him didn't have to scour. It was one thing to prepare the evening meal, but totally another to have to wash up as well.

Philip took the ice cream container out of the freezer and dished out spoonfuls into small plastic bowls. Ice cream contained milk, didn't it? A healthy treat. Too bad their mother wasn't there to stop him giving them sugar, frowned Philip. Big sugar, she'd say. Very bad.

Something was going to kill them in the end. What difference did cutting out sugar make? Why should he? What for? What for anything in this crazy out-of-control world?

He placed a bowl on each high chair tray and sat down at the table. 'Mummy will be home soon,' he said to his sons. He smiled at them, hoping they couldn't intuit his true frame of mind.

Everything will work out okay in the end, he comforted himself, though that remained to be seen. Their world had been turned upside down since a car had knocked Grace from her skateboard.

'Don't be naive,' he told himself. 'Nothing will be the same, ever again.'

Sebastian tipped his bowl up to drink the melted ice cream. Ethan did the same. Their plastic bibs caught most of the surplus.

Identical twins. Mirror images of each other. Philip poured another drink. He told himself he should be a better husband and father. He must lack something basic – must not have the ability to see the obvious. He should be more patient with his children. They didn't ask to be brought into this hard, cruel world. This stuffed-up place they'd be left with. He wouldn't frighten them with stories of climate change – the oceans rising, the ice melting. Terrorism. Trump. What disasters would his children have to confront?

The Homeless Girl unlocks the shed and leaves the burning building behind as she makes her way back to the open road. Who was it who said life wasn't meant to be easy? What's she to do in these situations? Perhaps it was an over-reaction, but the man had it coming. As she walks, the Homeless Girl removes her shoes to feel the grass, moist with dew, under her feet. Grounded on the earth. Just what she needs. Nothing comes easily. It's not as if this is the life she'd imagined for herself – on the streets and on the run.

*

Simon sat in the hotel bed and fiddled the dials of the sound system, trying to find some upbeat music, but what he kept coming back to was Pink, which seemed to be an annoying distraction to Rosemary.

Rosemary recognised the music from somewhere, probably from Grace's room when she'd go in to kiss her daughter goodnight.

Simon sighed. He wasn't a great fan of hotels. He found the room small, depressing and dark, and it smelt of the person who'd stayed there the night before.

He picked up the TV remote. Rosemary watched him fiddle around with the buttons. Even though they'd had a passionate session in bed already, she wouldn't mind going again. Simon had said, sure, if you want to go around the park again with me, that's fine. Just give me a few minutes.

She was happy to watch him as he found SBS On Demand and scrolled through the available movies. His face was soft and dimpled, fine featured, and not dissimilar to her own little boys, their cheeks so rosy and eatable.

She would like to kiss his body all over but she didn't know if that was overdoing things. He was interested in her curves and crevices, although she preferred to see his face when he was making love. Imagining that he'd had many lovers who'd wanted to devour his body, she accepted the fact that he probably had high standards of satisfaction that needed to be lived up to.

Simon put the remote down. He'd decided to give the movie idea a miss. 'Pretty woman,' he said, getting up to go to the toilet.

At first, she thought he meant her, but then she saw he'd stopped in front of a promotional brochure and was referring to Pink – the young hussy. Rosemary felt out of her depth. What was she thinking? Why would he find a woman like herself desirable? After all, she'd given birth to three children. As far as she was concerned, there was no harm in a one-night dalliance. It would do her good. It's not something that she'd be telling her family and friends. Not something to be proud of when her twins were at home waiting to be fed and her daughter flat on her back in a hospital bed while she watched a man struggle to open the bathroom door with his left hand.

She wondered why he didn't use the other hand.

'RSI,' he said dismissively and went into the bathroom.

She could hear him turn on the taps to run a bath. He'd said something about lighting all the aromatherapy candles to create a romantic atmosphere. They could have a good soak together in the tub, maybe order some champagne.

*

Later on, Simon had heard that *la Doctoresse de Anti-ageing* had rented out their apartment in the mountains above Nice and bought herself a small place in Monte Carlo. Or was it just outside Monaco? She must be raking in the money now she'd upgraded to an anti-ageing specialist. He knew the drill: enjoyable activities, change of habits, the link between diet and mood, the brain–gut connection. Then he'd heard it was definitely in Monte Carlo, near the casino, in fact, and she'd bought the place with that cocaine-sniffing, expensive-French-cologne-smelling *le Professeur*, maybe the same fragrance she'd bought him once. And Lawrence was calling the man dad. And then Simon had heard that *la Doctoresse* had left that man and had gone back to Nice and returned to their old apartment.

*

Julian and Dina are going for it in the granny flat out the back of Freda-from-across-the-road's house. In the area between the flat and the main house, Freda is picking up dead leaves from the grass. At least that's her plan. She's taking her time all too aware what those sounds mean. It's Julian, for sure. He'll keep coming over until he wins Dina back. She'll keep her mouth shut. An unfortunate image considering what she can see between the curtains. Her crazy friend Dina astride a kitchen chair, her red lips wrapped around Julian's rigid penis, her breasts exposed up and out of her brassiere, one hand in her nether regions. When it ends with a squirt over those fat breasts, Freda gropes along the grass to find another leaf, but forgets to bend at the knees and emits a groan. It is a long groan of disbelief. 'I've put my back out again.' On hands and knees, she makes her way back to the house.

*

Propped up against the pillows, Simon holds a square of chocolate between his fingers. He's about to bite into it when the television news reports: 'French President Emmanuel Macron treated Donald Trump to a meal at the famous Jules Verne Restaurant on the second floor of the Eiffel Tower.'

'Wow, look at that, Rosemary!' says Simon. 'Now that would be really something to have dinner in a place like that.'

'Mm. In your dreams.'

'Donald Trump seated himself next to Brigitte Macron. He told France's 64-year-old first lady in remarks that were caught on tape: "You know, you're in such good shape."'

'Women and their appearance,' says Rosemary. 'There he goes again.'

'Later, President Macron said he thinks he might have changed Trump's mind about climate change and that Trump may return to the table at the G20.'

'God,' says Rosemary. 'Will I ever see my darling Grace back at a table?'

'Hard to resist the charm of a French man,' says Simon as a chocolate drops unnoticed on to the pillow. 'My ex-wife could tell you all about that!' He picks up the remote and clicks the television off.

Rosemary suffers in silence from a broken heart beside him. 'Such a beautiful girl,' she says, thinking of her darling daughter Grace. Her voice is high-pitched, desperate, not like her at all. 'I used to be slim. My apologies. I used to play a lot of sport. My daughter, my firstborn, was petite too, before a car knocked her off her skateboard and her head hit the concrete.'

Simon takes the bottle from the wine cooler and sits it on the table beside the bed. He pours a glass of the expensive French champagne he'd ordered, hands her a glass and waits for her to say more.

Rosemary can't help herself; her mind races. She thinks of Grace lying silent in a hospital bed. She imagines Tinkerbell with a magic wand come to wave it above the girl and return things to how they were before, before the accident, and before all this. Rosemary sees the fairy dust enter the image that covers her daughter, repair the damage and take away the trauma that changed the biology of Grace's brain and struck her dumb.

Rosemary knows the world wants to escape into fantasy. It is a common response to the craziness, and she too would like to disappear into a place of the imagination. Rosemary likes to turn away from that which she is unable to face. She wants to close her eyes and be transported into another galaxy, and perhaps she is.

Simon hauls her back to planet earth. 'Feeling okay?' His face looms over her. He rescues the chocolate lodged between her hair and the pillow case. That look again. And his hair, Vaseline-shiny around a cow lick, upright at the crown like a cockie's plume.

Rosemary knows whose eyes are the same mix of blue and green. Narcissus? A person Philip would call 'impossibly good-looking'. So good-looking he can't be tempted away from his self-absorption. She can see it reflected in his face.

She imagines looking into Grace's blue-green eyes. 'Grace,' she whispers as she wraps her arms around the girl, so tight there is no room for anything to come between them until Grace is forced to utter the words, 'You're crushing me,' and pushes her away, but Rosemary won't let go. Rosemary holds her closer, determined to merge and never leave her side again and she doesn't, holding on and crying out, 'My darling.'

'No need to go overboard,' says Simon when he is able to climb off and lie beside her. 'Who is Grace?'

*

Julian walks alone at dawn through the steep gully of Cooper Park. Are there snakes slithering around after last night's rain? Dina had warned him about the snakes. Best to let them know of your approach. He treads heavily, his boots sinking into the muddy path. Julian sniffs his fingers, wanting to relive the excitement of last night. He rubs a shoulder that is still raw from her scratches. She's a wild one that Dina when you get her going. He had to tell her to move her face to the side so she wasn't screaming straight into his eardrum.

Julian feels the power in his legs as he strides along between the trees. His manhood is soaring with the birds: grateful, apologetic, transported. He hurdles the stairs two at a time.

Behind him, a woman with a dog on a lead talks enthusiastically to a face on the screen of her mobile. Her sister lives elsewhere and she misses her so much, loves to spend time with her more than anything in the world. She walks toward Julian, dragging her dog away from the murky water of the creek.

Julian stops at the top of the first flight of stairs and takes his camera out of his pocket and sets up to frame a picture. The woman's voice penetrates the moist air and disturbs the sound of the fast-flowing water over pebbles in Cooper Creek.

'Should I wait till you take the picture?'

'Oh no. It's okay,' says Julian. He motions for the woman to move past.

'Beautiful this time of the morning, isn't it? The best part of the day.'

'Yep.' Julian is thinking of capturing the woman and the dog from the back as they climb up through the gulley, to show the relative height of the trees.

'Immersing yourself in nature is the secret to a happy life,' she calls back to him. 'Make the most of it.' She smiles. 'See you.' And disappears in a gush of greenery.

*

'Relationships,' says Dina wistfully to Julian as she stirs the whey protein in to her mug of rice milk in the dull grey light of winter. 'I would be extra considerate if I were you.' Meaning: careful of what you say to me, who, because of your behaviour, has rented this tiny space with its fake wood cold lino flooring every panel of which I've paced across. I'm a relationship novice, that's what I am, so be very careful of the way you treat me.

'Don't you miss me?' says Julian.

'Yes. I miss your warm body on these freezing winter nights.'

Julian sits meekly; a naughty schoolboy who's just kicked a teacher in the shins and been sent to the headmaster's office to be disciplined. But maybe Dina has not given him the benefit of testosterone imbalance. Julian will try to explain why he lashed out at her that day and caused her to escape to this safe haven across the road.

'It won't happen again, darling. It was a temporary aberration – an anger issue.' Julian is doing his best to manage the anger thing. He gives himself permission to grab the curvaceous Dina and give her a squeeze. 'I mean, it's not as if I don't appreciate everything about you.'

Dina frowns. 'You mean you need me to do the bookwork for the business. Don't you?'

'Yes. That's true. I'd be lost without you.'

Dina's face falls all the way to her chin. An ability with numbers might be useful for a business partner but doesn't rate very highly on the intimate relationship scale, and true love is what she yearns for, it being that bit more satisfying.

'Compromise,' Julian says, 'compromise is what a partnership is all about.'

Dina remembers how things were in the first flush of their relationship, before they set up For Women With Curves. 'Things change.'

'That's when the compromise sets in.'

'Compromise?' But Dina doesn't want to hear the answer.

Julian has been thinking deeply about things, and doesn't want Dina to disagree. 'I don't know if I've told you my new idea,' he says. 'I want to launch an online plus-size bra retailer. It would tie in well with For Women With Curves.'

'You're joking?'

'I've been studying research about the increase in body fat. Breasts are depots for fat, and they've increased in size.'

'I'm so glad you've told me. It's funny. You know already everyone's bra size. My mum, my sister.'

'I thought you would want me to be upfront with you. The downside is it would mean six months of no pay.'

'No pay for six months! That's a big risk.'

'I can escape exorbitant Sydney rents by leasing a small Storage King. I can set up operations, have our computers next to the racks of bras. We'd go to work each day in a shipping container rather than our home office.'

How come he's ready to act so fast? Dina is dragging at the anchor and it's get it up quickly or he'll move on without her. She's sure of that.

'I'm asking you to support me with this,' Julian says and realises the words are coming out louder than he'd thought and tones it down. 'I'm asking – I'm asking for help so I can set up a new project. I'd give it six months. What do you say?

The kettle begins to boil. Dina is close to the boil too, which seems to suggest it is time to sit down with a cup of tea and unpack the details of this new development.

'I'd be crazy to ignore the huge gap in the market, don't you think?' says Julian, who knows a good opportunity when he sees one. 'I can become an expert on plus-size bras.'

'You want to shove me to the side, not be part of it?' says Dina softly. 'Looking at the profit and loss analysis for Women With Curves, we're doing okay.'

'It's only enough money for one person, and it's not growing by much each year.'

Her eyes welled. 'I thought you said we make a good team and that you love me.'

'Yes, I do. In my own strange way. You know I'm not much good at the intimacy thing. But that's not to say we still can't make a great partnership. I'd never give you the flick, sweetheart. We've both invested too much of ourselves already. I just want to take on this new challenge.'

'Let's just say you want to dump the clothing business on me and move on to greener pastures.'

'No. No. No,' protested Julian back-pedalling as fast his iridescent joggers would go.

'You are dumping me. You want to live separately so you're free to make a pass at every new piece of fluff that crosses your path. Think what it would do to sales if the word gets out.'

But Julian is beyond persuasion. All he sees is the macro trend showing women have larger busts these days. 'It's the estrogen-like substances in water bottles that get into the water circulation.'

Yes, Dina has read about that.

Julian doesn't want to fritter away his time on projects that aren't getting up quickly enough, no matter what Dina says about things taking time. Damn it. Julian just wants to get his teeth stuck into a new venture that is begging to be seized, with or without Dina. Unless of course North Korea's late-night firing of an intercontinental ballistic missile is more than a 'stern warning' for the United States. Something else to worry about. Best not to think about that, or he'll never have the courage to make a new start.

'I'm a doer, not a going-to-do,' he says, and goes out the door to get on with it.

*

Waking before daylight, Crystal lay anxiously in bed beside an empty pillow. She kicked angrily at the thick layer of blankets as a dreaded hot flush slunk up her chest, neck and face.

It was time to pull that no-good Simon back into line. She wasn't going to put up with his selfish behaviour and he needed to know it. How much longer could she be expected to wait while he reclaimed 'space' for himself?

*

The smack smack sound of balls bouncing off the walls of the courts at the squash centre.

The opposing team had arrived, a score keeper and umpire allocated. There he was, her growing-by-the-minute twelve-year-old Lawrence, representing the International School of Nice, warming up with cross-court side-stepping.

When the game started up, *la Doctoresse of Anti-ageing* leant back in her lime-green plastic chair. The tension was killing her. She took three deep breaths in and out against the spectacle of her son's ego being damaged by that big older boy. How could Lawrence be expected to see around that guy, thick as a tree trunk standing in the middle of the court? She dared not look away in case Lawrence sensed the withdrawal of his mother's loving gaze. It wasn't about win or lose, was it? What about personal best?

'He's playing well today, your boy. I can see a big improvement. All the kids have improved over the season. Look at my Tilly.' An accented voice, with a South American cadence.

She let her breathing return to normal. A head of touched-with-silver hair and matching closely cropped beard. A man with presence is how she'd describe him, sitting beside her.

'How they've all grown. Why, last season my Tilly was below my shoulder, now she's just under my chin.' He smiled widely, showing even white teeth. 'But you'd know all about that, wouldn't you? Your son has grown into quite the athlete. They were very happy to have him join the team. I keep a close eye on all the club competitions.' He moved a fraction closer to her.

All along the row of chairs on either side of them, parents yelled out words of passionate encouragement: '*Allez, allez vite*! Go on, go on quickly! Bend at the knees. What do you expect if you hit it straight back at him? Bounce on your feet. Just block the ball – he feeds off pace. Big comeback. Come on – you can do it.

'Those parents are projecting their own thwarted sporting ambitions on their children. Foul, isn't it, as Tilly would say. Her mother won't come to the matches. Finds it boring. Can you believe that?'

La Doctoresse de Anti-ageing nodded as the door clicked open and the competitors came out for a sip of water and words of correction from their coaches. She gave Lawrence a thumbs-up before he hurried down the stairs of the squash court to gulp water from the bubbler. Why didn't he bring his water bottle?

'You see. He won that game, against great odds. He's a strong player – quick around the court. He'll do well.'

'Mm.'

'Renaldo,' he said, extending a weathered but totally trustworthy, honest and reliable hand.

One thing she particularly liked was a firm handshake. *La Doctoresse de Anti-ageing* offered her own frayed-fingerless-gloved hand. 'Sarah.'

'Excellent.' He said this matter-of-factly, as though they'd known each other forever. Then he turned back to watch the second half.

*

At the end of the match when Lawrence took over as umpire for the next game, Sarah followed Renaldo down to the pro shop on the ground floor.

He turned as she scrunched up behind him over gym bags and squash racket covers, a chocolate ice block in each of his hands. He gave her one. After peeling off the wrappers, they saluted each other with the blocks of ice.

'*Bon appétit*,' she said and took a bite, totally forgetting that she never ate confectionery.

'Aussie, Aussie, oi, oi, oi,' blasted squash supporters at the world championships from the television high on the wall.

A curling of the upper lip indicated her embarrassment at the cringe-worthy sound of her compatriots' voices. Since living in France, the coarseness of some of her fellow Australians made her want to hide in a corner, but, like the ice block, it seemed she could tolerate anything this particular day.

This man was, she thought, like no one else she'd ever met. Or once, perhaps she'd known someone like him, before her life had changed so dramatically and she'd begun to see things more clearly. Immaculate, well-presented, elegant. All words that could be used to describe him. Rushing, harassed, uptight people like herself sat all around them dressed in tracksuits, scarves, jogging shoes.

'Great colour,' he said referring to her runners.

'Thanks. I bought them in Corsica in the summer.'

'My ex lives in Corsica.' He wore taupe leather lace-ups, navy trousers, lavender fine-knit jumper, sky-blue spectacle frames. His aquamarine eyes looked amused at the mention of this woman. 'Where do you live?' he asked.

'Villefranche-sur-Mer.'

'Charming.'

'It's close to my clinic in Monaco.'

'Oh really,' he said and scowled.

She wondered what he found disagreeable. Where did he live?

'Antibes.'

She could imagine him in Antibes. She'd been there, she thought. She had some memory of interesting laneways, a beach, expensive yachts, of getting lost trying to find the exit on the motorway and not being able to turn around and come back and all the time Simon had been cursing because he was hungry and they'd planned to meet a friend for lunch.

'Next Saturday is the open tournament and it will take place in Antibes. Lawrence could stay over with us and you could come on the train on Sunday morning and pick him up. My ex-wife will be staying over too. What do you think? Are you available?'

'Maybe. Well…'

She wondered what he'd think if she told him that by then she'd have told her ex-husband she missed him and wanted him back even though he was a selfish, inconsiderate bastard and a hopeless navigator.

'Sarah?'

How could she have been so crazy about him?

'That's a possibility.'

'Great. Fabulous.' Fabulous, in fact, was the word that best described this man.

Renaldo crossed to the railing and looked down on the courts. She went over and stood beside him. The two of them stayed there and watched the next squash pair warm up hitting back and forth across the court, getting ready for the rivalry in the next round of battle.

*

Still looking for Gypsy.

Rosemary drives around for hours, Rupert Brooke's poetry in a loop inside her head as repetitive as an ear worm. She parks the car under the sign 'No camping, no sleeping in vehicles in Cooper Park' and, overcome with guilt and worry, dry retches before making a dash into a toilet cubicle. Watching the water swirl clockwise down the bowl,

Rosemary comes to the realisation that perhaps the best place to be right now is back home with her husband and children.

*

Philip too must search the streets but not just anywhere, only those that lead to Cooper Park. As he drives, Classic FM keeps him company. When he stops in the car park, the music reaches a crescendo. Seeing the notes so clearly in his head, he writes the score in his mind and knows he can draw on it later.

Was it Shakespeare who wrote, 'If music be the food of love, play on?' He gets out of his car showing obvious signs of acute distress as a young woman watches. She feels for anyone who is sobbing and must offer him words of comfort and understanding.

'That's the way life is,' she says, and 'You win some, you lose some. Just open your eyes to the natural beauty around you, sir, and see it for the first time! Immerse yourself in nature. It's a great healer.' But Philip is not listening.

The young woman commences her walk up the gully from the car park, watching and listening for rainbow lorikeets, kookaburras and currawongs in the branches of the trees. She continues past the early morning tennis players in puffy vests and beanies but it seems this is her day to receive unwanted attention. Rather than have to empathise again as Philip had started on with more Shakespearean quotes, she hurried away and attracted the attention of a group of schoolboys intent on finding someone to victimise for their amusement by throwing stones from their hideout in the bushes.

Philip, perceiving an urgent need for a public convenience, makes his way to the toilets beside the courts.

For protection from their stones, the young woman takes shelter from the barrage in one of the man-made caves. The boys hammer small rocks on to the roof above her.

An elderly man who, having walked up the path with his dog, has seen what was taking place, hurries after Philip. Catching up with him, he takes his arm to stop him. 'Come with me. That girl needs our help.'

'I don't know the woman. I'm a pacifist,' he announces, with the emphasis on the fist. He knows from previous experience that saying something like that often leaves people speechless for a moment or two. And so it is this morning. He is pleased he is not to be drawn into a disturbance. He has enough of his own worries to deal with.

'Where's your sense of chivalry?' calls out the older man after him. 'No sense of social responsibility,' he tells himself as he makes his way to the cave to yell at those naughty boys to get on their way. 'No thought for others,' he says as he picks up the girl's abandoned styrene coffee cup which landed on the grass some metres away and throws it in a bin. He picks up a handful of stones. He stands angry and a little afraid. How come he gets drawn into the conflicts of others?

*

Even in sleep, the ghost of an 'I beat him' grin lurked between Lawrence's lips. Having tucked him securely into bed, the new squash racket beside him on the pillow, his mother was not able to do the same thing for herself.

She found herself pacing the apartment, sitting down, getting up, unable to settle in any one position. Her mind was not particularly focused on anything special, her head clear of its usual torments.

Her phone card lay on the dining room table in readiness for her call to Simon to tell him she has changed her mind and wants him back.

She went to the kitchen, cut off a wedge of Brie, stood at the window. What next?

She turned on the laptop in the study. She'd just check her emails and see what's happening on Facebook, she thought. She'd calm her restless indecision with some mindless scrolling on the internet.

*

In the men's toilet, Philip makes crazy deals and pledges. Philip does not usually hang around in public conveniences asking for help from the Power of the Universe. Desperate, Philip in his daggy corduroys, peaked cap askew on his head, leans against the porcelain wanting to make a bargain with a Higher Power: if his one and only daughter can be restored to her former self, or near enough to her former self, then he, Philip, will never complain about anything ever again, not even if he is unable to get another young adult historical fiction published.

Only once before has Philip taken part in such a bargaining process, though with not such high stakes. He imagines the moment now – a black and white image of a younger self in tennis shorts and white tennis shoes, he recalls. Yes, white shorts and white T-shirt gazing up at a full moon high in a black sky asking only that the universe allow him back on the court after his knee replacement; a tennis club full of gorgeous women in short pleated tennis skirts.

Was that when he first saw Rosemary?

If so, a toast to the Power of the Universe.

*

This need to stay on the run is a problem.

Why did things keep coming at her out of the blue?

Why her, why now, why her foster father?

The Homeless Girl smears gloss across her dry wind-chapped lips and, once they are moistened, goes in search of refuge from the rain and the cold in a warm shopping centre.

She rides the escalator up to the top floor and settles in to a couch to make use of the free WiFi. Though drug-fogged, she is not stupid and wants only to blend in with everyone else, but she expects to be tracked down all the same. She doesn't expect a happy ending.

She looks through the newspaper on the coffee table, hoping there are no Missing Girl stories or Wanted photos.

At first light, *la Doctoresse* makes her way along the foreshore that circles Saint Jean Cap Ferrat, her joggers collecting sand as she walks.

The moon drops behind the Alpes-Maritime. Along the waterfront, fishermen wait on the rocks, their rods reaching out into the Mediterranean, settled in early before the sun rises too far above the sea. The fish move silently below them, their flat tails visible between the boats.

As she walks, *la Doctoresse* remembers with dread her mother's rice pudding that she'd been forced to eat as a child, with its tasteless stick-in-your-throat texture. On that particular night, she had been feeling especially repulsed – she'd enjoyed the roast lamb with homemade mint sauce – but she'd had enough to eat and refused to bite into the dessert her mother had carried into the dining room on a large silver tray. Nothing from that day to this morning has ever tasted worse, filling her with dread like when she'd been forced to stay alone at the table until she'd eaten it all. She can experience it now, this being forced to do something that is not in her best interests. And why is she remembering it this morning? Because of the realisation that no one is forcing her to put up with that no-good Simon again. It's a choice thing. And no, it's not because of meeting Renaldo and the possibility of a more suitable romantic partner. For goodness sake, the man is only recently divorced. She's heard how the first woman to date a man after his divorce becomes the nursemaid. Much better to be the second girlfriend.

It is this business of forgiving herself. To have self-compassion for her struggles, an acceptance, for better or worse, for her failure to stay in the marriage to Lawrence's father.

The boats twinkle on their moorings. The sun is rising over the sea. She hears the boat bells. Sees the reflection of the sun on the water. She is attuned to the world around her again.

All that is left to do is not make the phone call to Simon.

She is ravenous. She is headed for the port to an early-opening bakery where she can order a croque-madame and short black. She doesn't need to reconsider. She sees now she is not an irredeemably awful human being. No more self-blame, guilt and regret for the separation. She plugs in her headphones. Piazzola's tango warms her solar plexus. Phew! It's not that she no longer expects to feel the guilt of breaking up the family unit. She knows it will reappear again. But she knows she can be free of it for days at a time, that the long periods of emptiness and longing have passed for now.

La Doctoresse rips up the phone card and lets the wind scatter the pieces into the sea.

*

The Homeless Girl is ravenous too. It's no surprise, the dark abyss of neediness eating away at her entrails. It's her karma, considering her unexpected, unwelcome status from birth. That's what the psychologists say, anyway. Will she always be in a state of crying out to be fed?

She hops over a fence and enters the back door of a garage. She rummages through bags of stuff stacked behind a BMW. Who knows? There might be something of value in here.

*

Rosemary and Philip walk towards one another with care mounting the crest of the hill. They stop and look into each other's eyes in front of the neatly trimmed hedge on either side of the gate that leads to Philip's handmade cobblestone path.

He pulls back the latch on the gate and motions for her to enter first. 'You didn't make it home last night.'

'I'm here now,' she says.

Philip presses past her. The rubber soles of his New Balance lace-ups scrunch noisily along the cobbles as he walks toward the front door. His shoulder skims the chipped stonework, liberating the sweet fragrance of the jasmine which grips it. Chipped-away-at is the phrase that springs to Rosemary's mind. But she'll not let her marriage be chipped-away-at any further, she vows, following him along the precious made-with-his-own-hands path.

'There's something wonderful about working in stone,' he liked to tell her, 'that sense of achievement when you make something that didn't exist before.'

She follows him in through the red painted door and into the house.

He pulls off his peaked cap and hangs it on the empty hat stand in the entrance foyer. He walks across the lounge room, through the arch-way to the kitchen and turns to face her.

He has nothing to say to her, but she has plenty to say to him, start-ing with 'You are my one and only,' her mouth and eyes naked in the harsh morning light, vulnerable without lipstick and mascara.

Philip nods, his balding scalp left bare without his cap. He leans down to straighten the door mat, his hands roughened by the building of the stone path, and picks up two postcards that have slipped through the flap of the letterbox. One from his cousin in Portugal, the other from their academic friends Jason and Claudia who are on a bridge cruise to Noumea.

'Who can be bothered to write postcards these days?'

'Exactly. Who sets the time aside for such things?' She takes the cards from him and throws them on the kitchen bench. She wants to hold her husband close. And she's desperate to tell him about the imperative she feels to get it across to their children the need to make time for those they love: the necessity to not let life's challenges stop them from slowing down and creating space, especially after her unsettling night with Simon, but maybe she should bring that topic up at another time.

'You spent last night with that guy from the poetry slam,' says Philip.

'You've got an overactive imagination.'

'I saw the way you looked at him that night at the Four In Hand. A husband knows these things,' saying the first thought that springs into his mind.

'I needed some time out. You know how it is.'

'Did you have company during this time out?' says Philip accus-ingly. 'Time out for one, or time out for two?'

'I wasn't entirely alone. There was the man at reception.'

'Did you break our wedding vows? Did you sleep with that man from the poetry slam?'

'I'm not into sleeping with strangers.'

'I want to know the truth. Did you break our wedding vows?'

'It's neither here nor there, according to some people.'

'I'm not some people. I want to know. And don't make up one of your stories. You know I can tell when it's a story.'

Rosemary has faith in her storytelling. 'Definitely not,' she says. 'I did not have sex with that man.'

*

Still looking for Gypsy.

The case worker from rehab parks her car behind a panel van and walks toward 94 Bunnerong Crescent. She can see smoke rising from behind the house. Gypsy the golden Labrador lies whining on the grass. His tail wags when he sees her. What's going on here?

The case worker knocks on the front door. The Homeless Girl doesn't appear to be home, and neither is anyone else.

She walks around to the back of the house to the shed. 'Anyone there?' she shouts.

She puts in a call to the fire department before peering in the window.

*

Simon hurries to the information desk at the hospital. Which room is Grace's? Simon has given the situation a lot of thought since his evening with Rosemary. Grace needs something to jump-start her out of silence. He's planning to tell her he's a friend of her mother's and he's discussed with her the possibility of Grace working on Saturdays in the soon-to-be-his hairdressing salon. He's prepared to take her on as a trainee. A job is what she needs. He could give her an apprenticeship when she finishes school. No need to give up hope. She'll be on her feet again in no time if she does what the physio says.

He knows the number of Grace's room and the floor. The doors of the lift close gently behind him.

*

Still looking for Gypsy.

'Shit a brick. Will you look at that?' says the case worker to no one in particular. She opens the car door for Gypsy to jump in before driving away with her.

*

Simon assumed a patient in hospital would be in their pyjamas, sick-looking, but Grace is lying on top of the bed, eyes closed, looking like any other teenager.

Last night in the hotel, Rosemary had told him about Grace's refusal to do the exercises to strengthen her legs so she can stand and walk. 'The whole thing is a living nightmare,' she said.

The nightmare continues, thought Simon, on and on until someone talks some sense into the girl.

He stood at the window and looked out over the tennis courts at the park, his mobile in one hand. The Eastern Suburbs tennis comp was taking place below him. He typed in his password on the phone and took a photo.

A man in doctors' scrubs was walking through the doorway into the room but Simon did not notice because he was wondering how to describe the sound a tennis ball makes to include in one of his poems.

The doctor went to the foot of the bed and checked the charts.

'Things are looking pretty good,' he said to Grace. 'You'll be home again in no time. Would you like that?' He bent down towards Grace's lips hoping to hear a whispered response.

Grace nodded and whispered something that only the doctor could hear.

'That's good then,' he said. 'No rush. When you're feeling up to it.'

There's only one sound a ball can make when being hit by a tennis racket, thought Simon, although there are many different words to describe it.

On the bed, Grace smiled at the doctor and then closed her eyes again.

Quietly, the doctor reached out and patted her hand and so, when Simon stopped thinking about composing a new poem and turned to say the things he'd come to say, he found he had missed his chance. Grace was fast asleep again.

*

Back at the centre, Kingston waited for Betty in her massage cubicle, and when she came in, smelling of patchouli, all the little aches in his bones told him this: she has been out to the dam with another man.

He inhaled the sweet fragrance of her neck and moved back. 'I want to know how long you've been showing another man our secret path through the bush?' he said purposefully, his voice sharp as a spear.

Worry contracted her face: her lips tightened, her eyes shrank narrow and alarmed. 'What makes you think I've been taking afternoon walks with –' she began to say. 'Well, just once or twice.'

He stepped away from her and marched angrily around the massage table, stroking the towels neatly stacked on the shelves, not prepared to hear another word from her. 'How could you?' he said. 'You know how important trust is to me!' He picked up a book – *Conversations with Remarkable Men* – next to the handbasin and banged it back down. 'How could you share our special walk? How could you be so dishonest?'

'I'm very very sorry,' she said.

'Yes. Well, so am I,' said Kingston. 'This is the end of us.' He could see it now, leaving the centre, heading out into the unknown again. Thumbing a ride to somewhere, to anywhere. 'I feel so utterly betrayed!' Everything around him lost its stability, moved under his feet.

Betty was quiet and he was quiet and then she began to speak, in a pleading way – there it was: the plead again, reverberating at the periphery of his life like a demanding child. 'We are both so lonely here at the centre,' she said. 'But I've been patient with you. That's all I've done for the last few months. I helped you get barista training, let you take your time to settle in, showed you another way to live without being forced to stay here as a volunteer in the kitchen.'

Kingston thought about Betty and the ways she had tried to show him she was on his side, her optimism and belief in him, always doing her best. The more he thought about it, the more he felt a fool, lacking in common sense, unable to see what was in front of his eyes. His anger winged away like a bird into the big blue sky. He felt as he had when his petty criminal father had at last grown stooped and old, spindly like a grasshopper, all arms and legs, unprotected by wisdom, just like Kingston's runaway teenage daughter, and Kingston had been left with his anger. There it was, unresolved and still in place. He would hug his mellowed father goodbye, his bones sucked dry, and think, where the hell were you when I needed you?

The healing power of distance, Kingston thought. What a joke.

Betty had begun to cry. She sat at the bed's edge and curled inward, her soft, smooth face in her small gentle hands, her head falling downward into the pastel flowers of her blouse.

He felt wobbly and turned towards the door. A wind had picked up and in the afternoon lit the sky as the branches of the trees gasped in the breeze, moving as one like a chorus of ballerinas. 'I've never seen you upset,' he said.

'Well, I hurt,' she said. 'I even cry watching the news. You don't really know me, Kingston. You don't give me the time to listen.'

But he could only continue to stare out the doorway, touching his fingers to the rolled-up white towels. He felt far away, as if he were back at the house he'd shared with Crystal and their teenage daughter, the one who'd taken off with the tennis coach. He'd walk around the neighbourhood at dinner time and catch glimpses of fathers come home from work to their families – the flicker of television screens and the smell of food cooking.

'We've found each other now,' Betty was saying. 'And in the various ways that a relationship can be negotiated, we can make a life together.'

Behind the meditation room, where the tree branches had stopped their restless gyrations, he saw the cumulus clouds ablaze in the setting sun. He turned, dazzled, and for a moment he thought he saw his runaway daughter's face in Betty's eyes, all the missing teenagers taken up habitation in her face, the ghost of his dead father dull like an overcast sky, and he went to them, to shield and enfold them, seeking to apologise: I did my best. 'Please accept my apologies,' he said.

And she whispered, 'Of course I will. Of course.'

*

'The thing is, I was a mistake,' says Kingston as they follow the bush path up the hill. And later, as they sit by the dam listening to the crickets, frogs and twenty-four varieties of birds, 'My mother thought she wouldn't fall pregnant while she was breastfeeding my brother.'

'That's what they told women in the olden days,' sighs Betty. 'And look how many unwanted babies resulted. Now stop talking and listen to the silence.'

'Yes. All that talking is exhausting,' says Kingston.

Betty puts an arm around him. 'It's good you realise that. You're a very wise man, though your brain chemistry needs to be fired up. None of that painful family stuff helps. One day, Kingston, you might go for some talking therapy and you'll find you don't need to keep searching for the meaning of life, you'll stop looking for answers and – oh Christ, Kingston, let's get going. That wind has picked up and it's bloody freezing.'

Kingston hops up ready to follow her back to the centre. 'We'll see,' he says jauntily.

*

Rosemary and Philip make their way up the stairs towards their bedroom. They would spend the morning there.

Ultimately, no new baby is conceived. Rosemary is far too advanced with the hot flushes, her eggs grown old. It is reassuring to them both that an unwanted pregnancy is no longer a possibility. Grace and the twins have given them more than enough to worry about.

Grace still sits silently since being run over and has not spoken to them since. The twins will never be allowed to ride a skateboard no matter how much begging goes on.

*

Madam Betty was trying to make out the road ahead through the morning mist but she could only see as far as the beams of the headlights allowed as they rounded the bends of the lower mountains.

'I only need to see as much as the headlights reveal. We'll still get to our destination. Just like life.'

'Why do they call the group In Search of the Miraculous?' asked Kingston.

'Well, they could hardly call themselves the Healing Power of Silence, could they? Besides, they love all that searching stuff.'

'What stuff?'

'At the seminars.'

'How do you know so much about what goes on at the centre?'

'I hear things in the corridors and at mealtimes'. Betty raised one hand from the wheel and numbered the items with her fingers. 'No stimulants. No smoking, no caffeine, no alcohol, no sex.'

'Really?'

'What's wrong?'

'No sex?'

'It saps your energy.'

'You probably don't know, but all those white-robed facilitators have their own large oil heaters stashed away in their rooms. They turn the power off at night in the dorms. That's why us volunteers freeze.'

'You've got to get an independent life, Kingston. Warn others of the perils of volunteering at a place like that. We can set up a home together. We'd get by, you know.'

*

'That's the way life is,' said Julian. 'Don't you agree?'

'The meaning of life and all that is somewhere I don't go,' lied Crystal. 'I had enough of those discussions when Kingston was here.' And thinks, I don't care if you and Dina split up. 'If you don't want to include Dina in your new business catering to the need for extra-large brassieres – due, as you say, to oestrogen in the water supply – you need to accept the consequences.' Anyway, I don't care. All I care about right now is indulging in some self-care. I want to lie back in a massage chair and have a pedicure.

'She's very upset with me,' said Julian. 'She doesn't want to keep going with the pyramid-selling side of things.' His eyes glistened. Oh, for goodness sake. Not self pity, is it? After all, he was the one who changed the lie of the land and started something new.

'Will the world come to an end,' asked Priscilla who'd been in the office alcove all along looking through Facebook, 'if America and North Korea fire at each other?'

Julian wiped his face with the sleeve of his shirt.

'There's a box of tissues on the bench, Julian.'

Julian sniffed loudly to clear his nose. He put an arm around Crystal.

Oh, no. Don't make a move on me. For God's sake.

'That's a disgusting noise,' said Crystal, though the last thing she wanted was to be teaching Julian good manners. 'Use a handkerchief.'

'Apologies,' said Julian slowly, and pulled a tissue from the box. 'I didn't mean it to be the end of Dina and me as a couple. I just wanted…' His voice rose in pitch, more confident now he'd decided it wasn't his fault: it takes two to tango. All he'd done was break the co-dependency between him and Dina. That's how he saw it anyway.

He sat there looking at Crystal.

Crystal hoped that would be the end of it, but she sensed he had more to say. She averted her eyes, not wanting to see the sad look on his face. Julian who used to think he was God's gift to women.

Crystal thought of that hot and humid morning when Julian had thought he'd left his mobile and had come over unexpectedly to have a look for it. He'd stood at the bathroom door while Crystal had looked out the window wondering what Simon was up to running down the back stairs, and suddenly Julian had been close behind her, had wrapped his arms around her and turned her to him and kissed her and they'd ended up on the floor in the hallway.

Julian had looked into her eyes as if trying to see how deep they really were. 'This was totally unplanned. Sorry.'

Unsaid thoughts had hung in the air.

'I'm happy you did. Priscilla has gone to a friend's house for a play date.' Crystal had reached down, run her hand over Julian's face. 'I've still got that special place in my heart for you, you know.'

'Sorry,' Julian had said, getting up. He stood over the partly dressed Crystal looking angst-ridden. There was embarrassment too, but who would know the reason? 'Dina's waiting for me. I'm already twenty minutes late. She'll be furious.'

Crystal had been confused. Seemed like Julian thought this was an innocent diversion. She'd felt used, naïve, as Julian, six feet tall and invincible, had walked to the door, where he turned and winked at Crystal.

'You shouldn't be standing around half dressed, you know,' Julian had accused her. 'It's very provocative.'

'What are you talking about?'

But Julian had been on the way to his car already. He'd stopped to give his mouth a rinse in the bathroom on his way out. Crystal had stayed on the floor in the hallway and listened to the water swirl down the drain. She'd pictured Julian in there using a finger to wipe toothpaste over his teeth before spitting out into the new square-shaped handbasin. The front door had banged closed. The car had started up out on the road. Vanished.

Then had come something else, a surprising low wailing which filled the hallway with a sound that had nothing to do with sexual gratification. Crystal had been devastated to listen to it but knew she wouldn't be able to put an end to it until it had exhausted itself. Who would have thought he'd take advantage like that?

'I'm sorry we're not continuing with the pyramid-selling group,' Julian was saying now.

'I'm not. It's not as if we made any decent money.'

'*We* did,' said Julian, which was true. 'That's the way those things operate. Sorry but –' He sniffed again, an involuntary sniffing.

Crystal would miss the camaraderie of the other women in the training group, but, in the grand scheme of things, it wasn't important. She had enough on her plate with holding down a full-time job, being a mum to Priscilla and keeping an eye on that slippery Simon. Once, she would have liked to discuss these things with Julian but now Crystal felt exhausted, wrung out from keeping her head above water, of earning a living, with no time to herself to practise self-care. She'd reached her limit. At least she had Simon on hand to shop and cook and take a turn with the childminding. Crystal suspected this resigned tone would fall on deaf ears with Julian, though her praise of Simon would piss him off. Crystal tried to think of a conversation stopper. She saw the *Sydney Morning Herald's* headline: 'The "new" greatest show on Turf'. The spring racing season must be approaching.

'You and Dina made money because you were on the top of the pyramid. Anyway,' said Crystal, her voice rising and hardening in an effort to get her point across, 'wouldn't you say in all fairness, Julian, that pyramid-selling has had its day? The thing is, sweetheart, we may have all moved on. Begun a new era of shopping online. Who can be bothered to host one of those Women With Curves parties? And who can be bothered to attend them, even with the free cocktails?

The sides of Julian's mouth dropped. 'Well, that's telling it the way it is.'

Just for a moment, Crystal saw the other six feet tall and bullet-proof Julian, last spring's version, standing at the door to the bathroom telling her how he couldn't help himself, but that was not connected with anything that was being said now, was it? She lifted Priscilla up from the office chair and sat her down beside her on the couch for support.

Priscilla resisted this fake show of female camaraderie. 'No thanks,' she said, jumping off the couch.

Annoyed with herself, she let Priscilla go back to the computer.

'There's nothing wrong with speaking out and saying the way things are. And, in fact, the others feel the same way. They're over it.' Crystal turned her defiant eyes to the *Sydney Morning Herald* as the wind through the window flicked the pages.

Julian adjusted his position on the chair. He seemed more in control of his emotions. Crystal sighed gently. Things don't stay the same for long.

Julian leaned towards her on the couch, looped his arm around her waist, pulled her closer. 'And what,' he muttered, 'what does the *Sydney Morning Herald* have to say about the fashions for the Spring Carnival? What do they predict as the latest for the track this season?' Julian nodded to himself then stood up ready to nod goodbye. He was heading off; off to his new digs in the old warehouse space, the kind of place, it was said, that trendsetters liked to snap up for renovation.

Crystal and Priscilla walked Julian to the front gate.

'See you later, alligator,' said Crystal in remembrance of their old schooldays. 'Or not.'

'In a while, crocodile. Or not.'

Crystal watched him hurry across the road to his car. She thought him light on his feet. Julian stopped at the big red letter box and looked back at Crystal. Priscilla swung on the gate, her elbows supporting her.

A grey sky hung low behind the line of jacaranda trees that led to the park. The dreamlike quality of the muted day blurred at the edges, like Crystal's heart as she pulled her cardigan tighter around her body.

'*Adios*,' she said, though by now Julian was definitely out of hearing range. Crystal noticed the birds flitting between the spring blooms of the jacaranda. Was Julian changing like the season, preparing for new growth?

And, if Dina was co-dependent, why had she changed the locks at home?

Life wasn't simple.

*

From his lookout across the road, Simon watched Julian get in his car and drive off. Simon despised Julian. Always had. Always would. Because Julian had been good at everything at school, on the sports field and in the classroom. Because Julian was able to pull the prettiest girls, the blonde Amazonians. Because Julian kept a record of his conquests and should have been expelled. And, to top it all, Julian had been the apple of his parents' eyes, parents who thought the sun shone out of his arse.

After seeing Julian that day at the gym when he and Dina were setting up a pop-up shop, Simon had hoped Julian might not remember the full story of his own dysfunctional family, but when he'd come home that night from Rosemary's house and seen the email that Julian had sent Crystal, Simon had known he hadn't.

It had all been there: all the old humiliations. Simon had wanted to laugh, it had been so long ago, but he wasn't able to. He'd deleted the email but had been unable to do the same with his emotions. The memories kept shape-shifting, turning themselves into vivid and painful images. Dad's story of becoming a manufacturer was clunking its way through a projector and its main character, his beret at an angle on his head, turned round and noticed his son who was coming to work with him in the school holidays, before turning back to watch the road. Was Dad crying? He who never cried; had he always felt trapped and unhappy as he drove for hours each day out west in his white Holden, one of Mum's corned beef and mustard sandwiches in the waxed bread loaf wrapper beside him?

But one day, Dad didn't make it home. They told everyone it was because of the slipperiness of the road surface after rain. Dad had said the long drive to and from the factory would kill him one day, only Dad had died with his head in a rope hanging from the rafters in between the rows of machinery, this being Dad's final desperate act after Mum's suggestion he pull his finger out and start making some real money so they wouldn't go bankrupt again. Only, Dad being Dad, he'd slit his wrists as well, just to show her he was able to do something really well if he tried really hard.

*

At the first set of traffic lights, Julian checks his phone.

What could he have been thinking of just now telling Crystal that losing Dina would be the end of him, when all the time he had the new challenge of the extra-large-brassiere online business? It would be Dina who was left with nothing. She'll be hopeless without him telling her what to do: making plans, arranging everything, driving her around. She doesn't have the living skills necessary to think ahead. Too passive. A result of all that dope smoking. No incentive. She hadn't been like that originally. But now she relied on him so much she'd be nothing without him.

A new challenge, though – a new business to get his teeth into would be different.

He really must come up with a name for the new online company. Something short and catchy that described its unique qualities.

Once he'd found a name and created a website, he'd have them painted on the back of his car.

*

The tennis courts in Cooper Park have been resurfaced. The night lights have been fixed.

Council workers advance in utes to weed the natural amphitheatre of the gully. Paths had been blocked by an overgrowth of weeds, fragile steps cracked and uneven, and foxes running rampant. The council was doing its best to maintain the place properly to unblock the streams by removing the build-up of dead trees that created a mosquito breeding ground.

Simon staggers out from behind the trees. He waits for the council trucks to grind past. When they do, he hurries across to find an image of his father lying on the road. 'You silly man. You shouldn't have thought you were a burden to us.' How could I have sided with Mum against you, me of all people, because, just like you, I've found out how difficult it is to earn a decent living. 'I'm so sorry, Dad,' sobs Simon. 'Please forgive me.'

'I'm sure he will, young man,' says an elderly fellow who is limping past. He holds a brown wooden cane and a dog on a leash. 'But I don't think apologising to a dead tree will help you out.'

'I wasn't talking to a tree,' protests Simon. 'I was just apologising to…it was my dad… He was…

'I must inform you,' growls the log, 'that I've always found you a disappointment as a son. Even when you were little, I knew you would never amount to much.'

'And I must inform you,' says Simon, straightening up and puffing out his chest, 'that an absent dad wasn't what I wanted either.'

'Of course he wasn't,' says the elderly gentleman, pulling on the dog's lead. 'Here, have a pat of Billy. It'll make you feel better.'

'I prefer cats.'

'Man's best friend, you know.'

Simon is bursting and forced to stop halfway down the road and urinate outside the Clifton's in between their car and the gutter.

Simon wonders why his father never bought him that dog he'd promised. He'd decided already to call him Pat the Dog.

Back in the lounge room, Crystal is trying to find out why Priscilla is laughing in a high-pitched tone and won't stop to talk or be calmed down. Crystal knows it has something to do with the *Sydney Morning Herald* because all Priscilla will do is fold it up into smaller and smaller pieces. At last, Crystal convinces Priscilla to give it to her.

'MEN'S SHED HORROR,' she reads quietly.

'Louder,' shouts Priscilla and moves in close beside her mother. 'She might get to hear you and come to see me.'

Crystal reads the front page to herself. About a teenager who has tortured a man in a shed then set the place on fire.

This is enough to send anyone into a state of hysteria, but worse still is Priscilla's insistence that this girl, this Amelie something-or-other, used to live down the road in Cooper Park and is, in fact, her big sister.

'But we don't know anyone named Amelie,' exclaims Crystal, knowing it is not a very good reason, but it's the only thing she can come up with for now.

'Her name's not Amelie,' sniggers Priscilla. 'She's the Homeless Girl, and she's been sleeping in the park all the time.'

'But princess, gorgeous girl, love of my life, listen to me. The Homeless Girl is not someone's name. It's just a description people use when they don't know a person's real name.' Who'd said this to Priscilla? Must have come from school. She'll have to have a word to those teachers.

'But that's who she is,' persisted Priscilla, jumping up from the lounge. 'It's her. She's the Homeless Girl, or else why are they putting a photo of her in the newspaper?'

'Because she did something really terrible and people want to know about it.'

'It's her. She's the Homeless Girl and she's my sister and she's coming back to find me. She said she would. She said one day I'm coming back to get you, sister, and then she sniffed that white stuff up her nose and lay down, only now she's up and about and coming to our house,' sang Priscilla and jumped back on the couch.

Crystal put an arm around her and held her tight. 'Have I ever told you anything that wasn't true?'

'Not that I know of.'

'I'm always straight with you, Priscilla, and tell you how it is.'

'I believe you.'

'This teenager is not your sister. I've got a photo of your sister in a box under the bed.'

Priscilla hops on Crystal for a piggyback up the stairs, putting a big strain on her mother's back, but they both enjoy these moments of mother/daughter bonding.

Crystal takes a child's birthday party photo out from under the bed and gives it to Priscilla. Crystal sits on the floor beside her daughter. Priscilla gasps and sighs repeatedly, and Crystal discovers she is overwhelmed with love for her little girl.

'I told you.'

'Can I copy and laminate it and put it on my wall?'

'Of course you can.'

Priscilla looks closely at the picture. 'She looks just like me.'

Crystal takes the photo from her. 'Yes. Exactly like you.'

It had been her eighth birthday party. Kingston had bought a pavlova base from the supermarket and topped the meringue with whipped cream, strawberries, blueberries, mango and passionfruit. In those days, Kingston liked to wear a big apron with the words 'Stay out of my kitchen' on the front.

'You disgusting man,' yells Mrs Clifton from the footpath.

Priscilla looks across at her mother and her mother meets her gaze.

'There's only one person we know who gets Mrs Clifton angry like that,' says Priscilla, and she's correct.

A key turns in the front door and Simon's back.

*

'I want a second chance.'

'You must be joking.'

'I'm sorry.'

'Me too. I'm sorry too.'

'We need to sit down and talk.'

'Not now. I'm too upset. We'll talk about it another time, but definitely not at the moment. I couldn't bear it.'

As things turned out, there was to be another time. Simon wanted forgiveness. Crystal was not surprised, considering what a mess he'd made of things.

'I was an idiot. A selfish unappreciative fool.'

Crystal agreed that was true. It wasn't as if Simon had shown any consideration for her and Priscilla and their life together, and it wasn't as if apologising would make everything go back to how it had been before.

Wanting to be open and perfectly honest, Simon tried again to explain himself. 'When was the last time you challenged yourself, and moved out of your comfort zone?'

Challenging herself was not a priority in Crystal's life. Getting Priscilla ready for school each day with a packed lunch in her bag was enough of a challenge.

'My mummy is the best mummy in the world,' said Priscilla, 'even though everyone at school says they've never seen her.'

Simon revealed his plans for the future and Priscilla moved in close to hear.

'I want to buy the salon. Give the place a facelift and sell the hair products online.'

It sounded a stretch to Crystal. The salon could do with a coat of paint, new basins, bigger mirrors, downlights. That is what Simon had to do to expand the client base and make a good living. Simon explained that marketing wasn't his strong point and he would need her help. If he made enough money, he could employ someone to answer the phone and make the tea and coffees. Could the Simon she knew and loved focus long enough to be a successful businessman? Could he give up his flirtatious eye and put his energy into building a business?

'I don't know,' said Crystal. 'I've been far too forgiving. You seem to think it's okay to do whatever you like whenever you like.'

'It's a bit of the pot calling the kettle black, isn't it? What about you and Julian? I saw him leaving the house.'

'Maybe I need to lift my game too. Perhaps our love has grown stale.'

'So you'll back me on this?'

'It's possible. Maybe I could do the accounts and set up a website.'

'The thing is,' said Simon, 'buying the salon is what I need to do. Take up the boss's offer. There'd have to be changes, though. I wouldn't be able to pick Priscilla up from school every day, and be the one responsible for all the shopping and cooking. The household duties would need to be shared.'

'Mm. That's a thought.'

'I'm afraid I'm a slow learner in life. I keep making the same mistakes.'

'At school, they say that you can tell who is a clever person. Clever people learn from their mistakes,' said Priscilla.

'You've always had a good head for numbers,' said Crystal.

Priscilla, to whom mathematics didn't come easily, rubbed her head. 'I dreamed your heart was removed from your body by a big black bird,' she said to her mother. It seemed something her mother should be made aware of right now.

Simon and Crystal began to kiss. They would keep going for a long time. Priscilla was aware of this. She let herself out the back door to play.

After a while, Simon sat up. 'You'll give me another chance?'

'As long as you behave yourself. No more mucking around. I know you can do it. Especially if you don't have all that spare time on your hands in the middle of the day.'

'I love you. I think you're amazing and I couldn't imagine life without you.'

'Compromise. Working out what you're prepared to put up with is the issue.'

'It will take time for me to prove myself.' Simon kissed Crystal again before going into the kitchen to find the champagne.

'Don't forget to unstack the dishwasher,' called Crystal, thinking how good it was to have an extra pair of helping hands. Someone who could peel and slice and chop.

Outside in the backyard, Priscilla was throwing a ball through a hoop attached to the wall. It was Crystal's old netball she'd brought back from Poppy's. 'Have you two made up yet?' she shouted, wondering if it was safe to come back inside. She hated seeing all that disgusting kissing stuff.

'There's a bottle of Prosecco in the fridge,' Crystal called into the kitchen, remembering the promised bliss of a couple of glasses of bubbly. And something to make Priscilla happy too. She supposed it wasn't too much to ask Simon to make a hot chocolate for Priscilla, and he said he would as soon as he made a toast to a new beginning.

'You'll have to make an appointment with the bank manager,' said Crystal, thinking of profit and loss, a business plan and high levels of financial stress.

'It's the three of us then?' Priscilla wanted to know as she jumped back on the couch.

'To the three of us,' proposed Simon as they clinked glasses.

We'll see how things unfold, Crystal thought, as she went upstairs to find her mobile, because now, at last, she could finally make an appointment for a pedicure.

It was a warm but overcast morning. The sun, climbing high above the eucalyptus trees, glided behind the clouds to illuminate the sky. Spring was crossing over into summer, the patches of sky above Cooper parklands flashing cobalt blue.

Gypsy, the golden Labrador, scampered and splashed through Cooper Creek, then shook himself dry. A muddy escapee. A barking survivor.

Priscilla saw him resting under a bench near the waterfall. At her approach, Gypsy wagged his tail excitedly. She patted his soft furry head and told him he could come and live with her now, so he followed her along the meandering pathway through the park back to her house to make a new home for himself under the family dining room table. Priscilla renamed him Amelie in memory of the elusive Homeless Girl.

Acknowledgements

Thank you to my writing community for much-needed feedback and encouragement that kept me motivated during the creation of *Lost in Cooper Park*.

Very special thanks to Susanne Gervay OAM and to Jan Cornall, who read, supported and gave invaluable suggestions.

Thank you to my beautiful, talented granddaughter, Natasha Sommer, who continues to give me editing advice and to support my work.

And thank you to my wonderful publisher, Stephen Matthews, Ginninderra Press.

9 781761 090424